"You're an exciting woman," he told her

Greg's face was inches from hers as he held her tightly.

"But you don't surrender too easily—or too often."

Susan pushed him away. "I have not surrendered at all!" she said forcefully.

He grinned. "I gathered that. So it looks like I'll have to revise my plans if I'm going to have any hope of achieving my intentions."

"Humph!" she snorted. "I can guess what your intentions are!"

Greg smiled. "There's one easy way to find out. Just relax, lie back, let me kiss you again, and I'll tell you all kinds of romantic things."

"I'm sure you've had plenty of practice," Susan said coolly.

"But not with a girl like you. So I've got to go back to square one and brush up some wooing techniques that have become very rusty."

DIANA GAIR
is also the author of this
Harlequin Romance

2519—HIGHLANDS RAPTURE

This book may be available at your local bookseller.

For a free catalog listing all titles currently available,
send your name and address to:

HARLEQUIN READER SERVICE
1440 South Priest Drive, Tempe, AZ 85281
Canadian address: Stratford, Ontario N5A 6W2

Jungle Antagonist

by

DIANA GAIR

Harlequin Books

TORONTO • NEW YORK • LOS ANGELES • LONDON
AMSTERDAM • PARIS • SYDNEY • HAMBURG
STOCKHOLM • ATHENS • TOKYO • MILAN

Original hardcover edition published in 1982
by Mills & Boon Limited

ISBN 0-373-02530-0

Harlequin Romance first edition February 1983

CHAPTER ONE

THE steamy Singapore heat rose in humid wraiths from the rain-washed concrete outside the Mandarin Hotel. One of the city's frequent tropical downpours had ended abruptly and Susan York had sweltered it out in the Tiger Tours minibus, trapped by the sudden deluge. She'd sat in the driver's seat, hot and sticky, with the windows tightly closed to keep out the lashing torrent that penetrated the tiniest opening and virtually brought traffic to a standstill.

She had parked as close to the hotel as possible, but if she had tried to run from the minibus to the entrance she would have been soaked in the first few yards. Now the teeming rain had stopped as suddenly as it had begun, and traffic started moving again. Susan opened the door and slid from the seat to the road, her white linen skirt riding to her thighs as she did so. There was a flash of long shapely legs before her feet touched ground when she straightened up and quickly tugged her skirt down.

She swept honey-coloured hair from her face, then glanced up at a tall, dark-haired man who was studying her coolly. He wore a tailored safari suit and as he looked at her perspiring face, she saw annoyance in his deep grey eyes.

Susan tossed her damp hair and glanced coldly at him, then slammed the minibus door. She made to stride past, but he thrust out a muscular arm. His actions were unhurried—and irritatingly confident, she thought, prickling angrily.

'I'm Greg McKenzie,' he said curtly. 'And I don't get any prize for guessing you're from Tiger Tours.'

Both sides of the ten-seater minibus were painted with the leaping Malayan tiger that was the company's logo, and the name was lettered on the front and rear of the bus.

'Oh!' Susan said shortly. 'Then it's you I've come to pick up.'

He nodded, and she saw even white teeth and firm lips above a determined chin that looked like its owner was used to getting his own way. His dark hair was crinkly and his muscular arms in his short-sleeved, bone-coloured safari jacket were deeply tanned.

The open-necked jacket showed the strong column of his throat and above the top button of the jacket there was the suggestion of more dark hair. His rugged features and powerful build in his tropical gear reminded Susan of a big game hunter. As she looked up at him she thought he was an unlikely male to want to take a conducted tour of Singapore.

She held out a slim hand and he gripped it briefly. She said, 'I'm Susan York, from Tiger Tours. I'll be taking you round this afternoon.'

One dark eyebrow rose slightly as he studied her lissom figure in its short white linen skirt and open-necked blue cotton blouse which she had unbuttoned for coolness while she had been trapped in the steamy bus. She coloured under his gaze and hastily did up two buttons on her blouse, concealing the swell of her bosom.

He said shortly, 'It's about time you got here. You were due at two o'clock.'

She sucked in her breath. 'I know. And I was here just after two. But I was stuck in the bus until the rain stopped. Tiger Tours are not responsible for the weather.'

He nodded as if he doubted her, then said, 'I didn't expect an English girl as my guide. The Chinese or Malays seem to do most of the tour driving.'

Susan said tersely, 'Normally I don't drive. I'm a tour conductor on our Malaysian trips. But we're short-staffed today, so it meant calling me in from my day off—or else cancelling the tour. And Tiger Tours *never* let their clients down.'

He grunted. 'Only keep them waiting for an hour.'

She flushed, then gritted her teeth and wrenched open the rear door of the minibus. 'Would you like to get in?' she snapped, her blue eyes flashing.

'Do I have to ride in the back?' he asked. 'Doesn't first come get to ride up front?'

She hesitated, then shrugged. 'All right. You can sit beside me if you want to.'

He said coldly, 'Very graciously put.' But he made no move to board the bus.

Normally she would have walked round to the passenger side and opened the door for a client, but she'd opened one door for him and she wasn't going to open another. She slammed the rear door shut, then opened the driver's door and began to climb in, leaving him to get aboard himself.

He stood and watched until she had settled herself behind the wheel, raising her self from the seat so she could pull her skirt down. She glanced at him pointedly and he slammed her door shut.

Viciously, Susan turned the ignition key and the starter motor whined, but the engine didn't fire. She tried again, several times, conscious that Greg McKenzie had walked round in front of the bus and was now climbing into the seat alongside her.

He settled himself comfortably and adjusted the seat to make space for his long legs. She could feel his gaze on her, but he made no comment as she repeatedly turned the key to start the reluctant engine.

She felt herself perspiring in the steamy tropical heat and she longed for the relief of the air-conditioning once the engine was running.

He said, above the noise of the whirring starter, 'You're going to flatten the battery if you keep doing that.'

Susan gritted her teeth and swept her hair from her damp brow as she kept the ignition key pressed down with her other hand. 'It's an old bus,' she said shortly, 'I've never driven it before. But our mechanics do look after them.'

He said easily, 'It's nothing to do with maintenance. It's more likely water in the ignition. You'd be better opening up the hood and letting the sun dry things out.'

Susan ignored his advice. Stubbornly she kept turning the key and the motor whirred and whined protestingly.

Casually Greg McKenzie reached across and put one strong brown hand over hers, preventing her from pressing the key. She turned and glared at him, then tried to shake his hand off. But he tightened his grip.

'Leave it,' he said, coldly and very firmly. 'Pull the hood release, then I'll get out and open up.'

She sucked in her breath, then exhaled with a slow hiss. He freed her hand and reached across her stiff body and found the hood release which he tugged open.

He withdrew his arm, which brushed across her bare knees, and she jumped at the contact. He got out and went round the front of the bus. In silent exasperation Susan pounded the dashboard then got out and stalked round to join him.

Greg McKenzie soon found the source of the trouble. He obviously knew his way around motors, for he quickly undid a part of the ignition system, then pulled out a handkerchief.

'The contacts are damp,' he said briefly. He blew on the ignition contact and wiped it with his handkerchief, then blew on it again. He replaced the part, straightened up and slammed down the hood.

'O.K.,' he said, 'now give it a try.'

Susan took a deep breath and walked stiffly round and got back in behind the wheel. She half-hoped that the bus still wouldn't start. It would be nice to show this over-confident American tourist that he could be wrong!

But when she turned the key the engine fired

within seconds and she was aware of him getting in next to her.

'Thanks,' she said shortly, not looking at him.

He grunted something and she concentrated on steering the bus out into the teeming Orchard Road traffic. Finally, when she got into top gear and the bus was humming along as smoothly as possible in the dense traffic, she turned on the air-conditioner and welcome coolness flooded the cabin. She hadn't turned it on earlier, for the engine was under-powered and tended to stall with the load of the air-conditioner until it was running at speed.

'You got more people to pick up?' he enquired. 'From other hotels?'

Now that she was cooling off, Susan's normally sunny disposition was returning. After all, the man was a client, so she'd better be pleasant to him. And he had got the bus started.

'Yes,' she said, 'only two people—at the Shangri-la. This is not one of our busier days. But still, three people will just about meet expenses.'

'And as you said, Tiger Tours never let clients down.'

'No, we don't,' she said severely. 'David Farrell—he's the owner, or part owner anyway with Mr Koh—says we run on time whatever happens. Even if there's only one passenger, we don't cancel.'

Traffic in the central city area was heavy. It seemed as if all of Singapore Island's two million people were on the roads at once. Susan had to concentrate on driving the unfamiliar bus, which was bigger than the little Datsun she regularly drove. Greg McKenzie glanced at her knitted brow as she concentrated on changing gears—something she didn't have to do on her own small automatic.

He didn't say any more, but glanced out at the cosmopolitan Singapore scene as it returned to life after the lashing downpour.

To make conversation, Susan said, 'I suppose driving on the left side of the road seems funny to you?'

He nodded. 'Nearly as funny as having the steering wheel on the right-hand side. But you're English, aren't you, so I guess you're used to it.'

Susan said, 'Yes, I'm from Dorset, although I've been here for three years. And what part of America are you from?'

'Los Angeles. That's on the West Coast.'

'Yes,' she said, 'we get a lot of Americans on our tours up into Malaysia.'

She changed down suddenly, baulked behind a truck loaded with Malayan pineapples, its exhaust belching diesel fumes.

'He'll be in trouble,' she said, 'blowing smoke like that. The government is very pollution-conscious.'

Greg McKenzie glanced out at the rain-washed street. 'It sure is a very clean city. One of the cleanest I've been in.'

Susan nodded as she changed into top gear again. 'Yes, the streets always look freshly scrubbed. You won't find any litter lying around. Even to drop a dead match in the street can bring a fine.'

He said, 'I haven't been here before. But I always thought of Singapore as a pretty dirty place.'

'It was in the old days, but not any more. Now it's the cleanest city in Asia. Which is just as well, since it's almost on the Equator.'

Unconsciously, Susan had adopted her tour guide's voice as she recited the standard facts about Singapore. She glanced at him to see how he was reacting and he looked at her expressionlessly.

She flushed slightly and said, 'If you don't want to know all about Singapore then just ask me about things you're specially interested in and I'll answer.'

She changed down to take a corner, then changed up again and accelerated. He said nothing.

She took a deep breath and asked, 'What kind of business are you in?'

'I'm in the export business,' he said briefly. Then he changed the subject. 'This entire street seems to be lined with hotels.'

She nodded. 'Yes. And they desperately need more visitors to fill them. And Tiger tours could do with more tourists too.'

'Business been bad?'

'Well, today will give you an idea. Only three bookings for this tour. And we haven't been getting big loads on our Malaysian tours either. So David—David Farrell—has a few problems at the moment.'

Greg McKenzie nodded. 'The tourist business has its ups and downs, I guess.'

Susan turned the bus into Orange Grove Road and when they reached the Shangri-La she parked, then excused herself while she hurried into the sprawling luxury hotel to pick up the couple who had booked on the tour. But when she came back she was alone, and Greg McKenzie raised an eyebrow enquiringly.

She said resignedly as she climbed into the driver's seat, 'Well, this is a one-passenger day. My couple cancelled—the wife has an upset tummy. So you're going to have an individual tour of Singapore.'

He grunted. 'Tiger Tours sure won't show a profit on this trip.' He glanced at her as she started the engine. 'I can cancel if you like. I can do the tour another day.'

She looked at him, surprised, then she said firmly, 'No—thank you. But David wouldn't like it if I agreed to that.' She put the bus in gear. 'So— off we go.'

He relaxed in his seat and commented, 'This David—the owner—is he your boy-friend?'

Susan turned slightly pink and silently cursed the handicap all fair-skinned people seemed to have of blushing or flushing at any personal question.

'Yes, I suppose he is.'

His tone was cool as he gazed at her. 'You suppose—or he is?'

'Well, yes, he is. He's a very nice person.'

'You planning to marry him?'

The pink on her cheeks became red. She said shortly, 'He's asked me a few times.'

'But you're not sure about it? Is he English too?'

'Yes. But he's been in the East for years. He likes it here.'

'And you don't?'

'Well——' Susan knitted her brows, 'I'm not sure. I loved it when I first came here three years ago. But I think I've perhaps had enough. I'd really like to go to Canada. Naturally I'll always be a foreigner in Asia—although I love the people here, especially since I learned to speak Malay.'

'And David—does he want to stay in the East?'

'Well, not necessarily. He'd probably be happy to go to Canada and start a new life. He's only thirty. But he doesn't want to go back to England—and neither do I. It's too cold, among other things.'

'Can't he sell out and go to Canada?'

Susan frowned as she swung the bus around one of the city's roundabouts. 'It's not that easy. Since the tourist business slumped there aren't many buyers about. K.K.—that's K. Koh, David's partner—would like to buy him out. But he's not offering David very much for his share.'

'So you have problems,' he said, his voice neutral.

She sighed. 'Yes. A few.' Then she shook her head vigorously. 'But I'm not supposed to be giving you my troubles. You've paid for a tour of Singapore—or as much of it as we can see in an afternoon. So let's get started.'

'Where are we going?' he enquired.

'We usually start with Sentosa—most tourists like it.'

'What's there?'

'Well, Sentosa is an island that had a long history of piracy in the old days. It was called *Blakang Mati* until recently. That means Behind Death, so it was a really rip-roaring place. But it's been renamed Sentosa—which is Malay for tranquillity or peace.'

'And what happens on this island of tranquillity?'

'It's actually a man-made tourist resort. You know—restaurants, swimming, boating golf course—kind of a playground.'

'Sounds terrible,' he said bluntly. 'I guess it appeals to the locals, but you can see that kind of place anywhere in the world.'

'Oh?' Susan took her foot off the accelerator and let their speed drop. 'Well, all right, we can skip Sentosa. We can go to the Jurong Bird Park instead. You might enjoy that.'

'What's it like?'

'It's a big park—man-made again, I'm afraid—with a huge cage full of birds—all very exotic.'

'That doesn't exactly grab me either. I'd like to see something more typical of Singapore—you know, its history, that kind of thing.'

She frowned. 'That's not too easy, Frankly, nearly everything in Singapore is man-made—designed for tourists.'

He shook his head. 'I guess I'm a lousy tourist. The regular attractions don't excite me. I prefer seeing things that are unique to a place, like anything that's left of the old Singapore.'

Susan found a parking space and pulled the bus into the kerb, then stopped. 'Well, the only place I can think of is the original old Chinatown—or what's left of it. It's gradually being pulled down, in the name of progress, but there's still quite a lot left just like it was a hundred years ago. It's not unique—other cities have their Chinatowns too—but I think Singapore's is less changed than most.'

He grunted. 'That sounds better. So let's settle for Chinatown.'

Susan said, 'All right, so our first stop will be the Temple of Heavenly Happiness. Is that exotic enough?'

Greg McKenzie nodded. 'I'll settle for that.'

She concentrated on driving through the narrow streets and when they reached Telok Ayer she managed to find a spot in the teeming street where she could park. When they got out, she locked the bus carefully.

'You have car thieves around?' Greg McKenzie queried.

'Yes, although it's a fairly honest city. But down here it's best to be careful. You certainly wouldn't want to leave anything lying in an unlocked car. That would be asking for it to be stolen.'

Without realising it, Susan had raised her voice to speak over the clamouring din of Chinatown and its closely-packed humanity. She rather liked Chinatown. Many tourists she had escorted had told her it was more Chinese than most Chinatowns. Certainly it had hardly changed since over a hundred years ago when Cantonese, Teochius, Hokkiens, Hakkas and Hailams had swarmed into the trading city. From the provinces of China they had brought their varied dialects, and their own gods whom they still worshipped. They had also brought the babble of noise that was typical of any truly Chinese town.

As Susan threaded her way through the narrow streets they were deafened by the jangling brass of a band playing at a funeral procession to scare away evil spirits. This met vocal competition from hawkers crying their wares, and the tapping of bamboo sticks which some traders used to proclaim what they were selling. The tapping was done in a code, meaningless to the uninitiated, but to the Chinese as familiar as an advertising jingle.

The cries of salesmen mingled with constant hammering from the shophouses where craftsmen worked half inside their shops and half outside on the sidewalks. There were carpenters, gold beaters, coffin makers and metal workers—many using modern electrical machinery, others pounding away with hand tools creating everything from washbasins to necklaces.

But above all there was the sound of a thousand transitor radios. Almost every tumbledown shophouse had at least one radio, some tuned to Western music but many to stations broadcasting wailing Chinese love songs.

Greg McKenzie was forced to bend his dark head close to Susan's blonde one to make himself heard above the din.

'This seems authentic enough,' he murmured. 'You won't hear sounds like this in a supermarket.'

She smiled. 'I like the colour as much as the noise. It's all very gaudy, but it's also very vital and alive.'

She waved one hand at the endless colourful banners that hung from almost every shopfront.

Ideographs in Chinese characters screamed at them in brilliant gold and violet on backgrounds of red and lime.

She asked, 'Do you like Chinese food?'

He nodded, drawing her aside to avoid a passing trishaw—pedalled dexterously through the throng by an ancient Chinese with wiry brown legs like wrinkled leather.

'Yes. And I wouldn't mind eating some. I missed out on lunch today. I had to go to a reception where they offered me endless liquor, but no food.'

'We can stop somewhere where you can eat,' she said. 'I'm not hungry, but I'll have tea with you.'

'A snack will do,' he said, 'and there doesn't seem to be any shortage of eating places.'

The smell of foodstuffs mingled with charcoal smoke, drying washing hanging from every house, smouldering sandalwood, paraffin, incense and a lot of dirt and sweat from the close-packed humanity.

Susan wrinkled her nose. 'You certainly know when you're in Chinatown! It smells like no other part of Singapore.'

Greg nodded. 'I quite like it. It's real—not something synthetic turned on for tourists.'

Susan stopped in front of a small open-fronted café with a few tables and rickety cane chairs on the sidewalk.

'This is a good place,' she said. 'I've eaten here before. It's called Fatties. The owner is actually Ah Fat, but he doesn't mind.'

Greg nodded and followed her as she threaded her way through the tables and into the tiny café.

A chunky, roly-poly Chinese in blue cotton trousers and a white vest came from the kitchen to greet them. He beamed at Susan and said, 'Hello, Miss Susan.'

She smiled at him. 'This is Mr McKenzie from America. He's a little hungry, but I'm not, so I'll just have tea.'

Ah Fat said hello to Greg, then led them to a table away from the noise of the kitchen where it sounded as if ten cooks were battering the carcasses of fifty chickens. He handed Greg a very creased and well-thumbed menu. Greg took it and glanced at its contents. All the dishes were in Chinese characters, with only the most cryptic English translation.

Greg said, 'I only want a snack. What do you suggest?'

Susan took the menu. 'Well, how about some fish rolls in sour sauce—they're delicious. Then perhaps a couple of sticks of satay prawn, and maybe some stuffed crab claws. Then——'

Greg held up his hand in protest. 'That sounds fine!'

Susan smiled and beckoned the hovering Ah Fat and gave him the order, adding tea for herself. Greg said he would have a beer and Ah Fat bustled off and began screaming at the kitchen staff, who screamed back just as lustily. Within a minute came back with Greg's beer and Susan's China tea in a small pot with a tiny bowl with no handle.

Greg drank some beer, then asked, 'How long did you say you'd been in the tours business?'

'Three years. I left England on my twenty-first

birthday. I met David when he was on leave in London and he offered me a job, so I jumped at it. England is pretty boring these days and this seemed more—adventurous.'

'And has it been—adventurous?'

'Well, not in Singapore. This is like any big city really. But it's different in Malaysia. It's virtually unspoiled—masses of jungle and miles of rubber plantations.'

'Sounds interesting. There aren't many unspoiled parts of the world left—that you can get to easily, anyway.'

'Malaysia is still one of them. Our tours go from south to north and get right away from the cities.'

He nodded. 'And what did your folks think of their daughter going out East?'

A shadow crossed her face. 'Actually, my mother is dead. She died when I was quite small. My father brought me up—although I spent most of my time at boarding school. Then I worked for a travel agent in London for a while until——' her voice tailed off.

'Until?' Greg prompted.

She forced a smile. 'Until my father married again.'

'And you didn't like his new wife?'

'No, I didn't. So I was glad to get away from England.'

He nodded, then Ah Fat bustled in with the food.

Greg tried one of the tiny fish rolls, then said, wiping his mouth with a paper napkin, 'You're right, they're good.'

Susan smiled and sipped her tea.

'What kind of things do you export? Have you found a market here for them?'

He finished a crab claw and wiped his mouth, then took a pull at his beer. 'Not yet. But I've only been in Singapore a couple of days. I'll probably have a look at Malaysia. It sounds more like the kind of place I'm interested in.'

'You could take one of our tours,' she said, then added quickly, 'I'm not touting for business. But they're a good way to see the country quickly.'

'How long do they take?' he asked, picking up a stick of satay prawn and nibbling.

'Only five days. And that takes you from Singapore to Penang by coach, then you fly back to Singapore—or on to anywhere else you want to go.'

'I'll think about it. As I said, I'm a lousy tourist and I'm not sure I could stand five days in a coach.'

Susan sipped her tea. 'The coaches are pretty comfortable, air-conditioned and all that. The distances aren't very great, so we spend most of the time in places like Malacca, Kuala Lumpur, Ipoh Khedar and Penang.'

'And you'd be the guide?'

'Well, it depends when you wanted to go. I take a tour out the day after tomorrow. We leave every two days. The next one would be conducted by Tanya Vorchek—she's the senior tour conductor.'

And nasty too, Susan added under her breath.

Greg glanced keenly at her. 'So you don't like Tanya much?'

Susan coloured, annoyed at the transparency of her thoughts. 'I didn't say that.'

He grimaced. 'You didn't have to. I could see it in your face when you mentioned her name. What's the matter with her?'

Susan tossed her head. 'Oh, she's very glamorous—exotic, in fact. But she's also very good at her job. She speaks about four languages, apart from English.'

'Hmm. That doesn't explain why you don't like her.'

Susan hesitated. 'I don't really know why I'm telling you all these things. I did start off by trying to get you to talk about yourself. You haven't told me anything about yourself yet.'

'I'm not very interesting. Just a businessman.'

'Obviously a successful one. You didn't even enquire the price of our tours. Most people ask that first.'

He grunted. 'I guess the price of a tour won't break me. I visited Tokyo before getting here—and you'd need to be a millionaire to afford Japan these days!'

She smiled. 'Everybody still thinks all American tourists are millionaires.'

He nodded. 'Well, this one isn't. Although let's say I'm not starving. But you've avoided my question—why don't you like Tanya?'

Susan forced a smile, slightly annoyed at his persistence. 'Well, just let's say she's rather well in with K.K.—Mr Koh. So she gets preferential treatment.'

'Hmm. You mean she's his girl-friend?'

Susan nodded.

Greg said, 'So what's wrong with that? You're David's girl-friend, aren't you? So that gives each of your bosses his own girl, eh?'

Susan coloured slightly. 'Well, Mr Koh is married and David isn't. Apart from that——' she hesitated and her colour turned to a flush, 'I—I——'

'You don't live with David, is that what you mean?'

'Of course I don't!' she said sharply. 'I live by myself. I always have,' she added tersely, looking straight into his enquiring eyes.

'O.K., O.K.,' he said shortly, placing one hand over hers. 'I wasn't prying.'

She snatched her hand away. 'You were!' she snapped. 'I mean, I haven't asked about *your* personal life—whether you're married, or have a girl—or girls.'

He grunted. 'I'm not married and I don't generally have girls. Girls plural, that is. One at a time is enough. I did have one special girl, but it didn't work out. So is that O.K.?'

His grey eyes studied her, almost mockingly, and to avoid his gaze she busied herself pouring more tea.

He was a very irritating man, she thought. She'd known David for two years before he had asked such personal questions as this American had after less than an hour's acquaintance.

She toyed with her tea while Greg finished most of the food on his plate. Then he sat back with a satisfied sigh and took a pull at his beer.

'That feels better,' he said. 'I always get just a mite touchy when I haven't eaten for a while.'

He smiled for the first time since she'd met him, and she thought he was really rather attractive when he let his expression relax.

She returned his smile. 'Most men are like that. Feed the brute—every woman learns that.'

He said gravely, 'I'm pleased you know the second rule of a happy marriage. You should make a great wife, some day.'

She flushed and lowered her eyes quickly and picked up her tea cup. There was no way she was going to ask him what the first rule was. Instead, she said, 'We can go if you're finished. I should get you back to your hotel before the peak hour traffic. It really becomes bedlam then.'

'O.K.,' he said. He signalled the hovering Ah Fat, who brought the check which Greg paid.

Outside, they walked back towards where Susan had parked the bus. They strolled along Sago Street, past the shops of the coffin-makers, and when they reached the minibus Susan walked round to the driver's seat and unlocked the door. Greg went to the passenger side and waited for her to open his door from the inside.

Suddenly he called out, 'Hang on a minute. You've got a flat tyre on this side.'

'Oh, no!' Susan cried as she hurried round to join him where he kicked gently at the front tyre. It was flat all right.

'Blast!' she exclaimed. 'This isn't my day!'

'I'll fix it,' he said. 'I hope you have a spare. It should be in the back somewhere.'

Susan said, 'No, you don't have to do that. I'll phone the office and they'll send out a mechanic. I'll get a taxi for you and pay your fare back to your hotel.'

'Rubbish,' he said forcefully. 'It'll only take a minute.' He held out his hand. 'Give me the keys and I'll find the spare.'

She said hesitantly, 'But you'll get dirty—your clothes, I mean.'

He grinned as he prised the keys from her reluctant grasp. 'I never got round to telling you, but I used to be a truck driver. And a coach driver too. So I've changed bigger tyres than these, without getting very dirty.'

She let him have the keys and he opened the door, then climbed into the bus and went to the back where he found the spare under its cover. He rolled the wheel out on to the road, then went back and found the jack and wheel brace.

'O.K.,' he said, kicking the spare wheel. 'There's air in it. So let's see where the jack fits.'

He knelt down and peered under the chassis until he located the jack lock under the door, then he started work.

A crowd of onlookers quickly gathered, most of them grinning, brown-faced Chinese urchins who chattered away in high-pitched voices. A few hawkers also stopped to watch the big white man working, as did some coolies.

Susan watched Greg with as much interest as any of the Chinese. He had the bus jacked up and the wheel with the flat tyre off in a few minutes. Then he straightened up, perspiring in the clammy heat, and glanced at his soiled hands.

'You're right,' he said, 'I'm going to get some dirt on me. And I'm starting to sweat. Would you like to undo my jacket and take it off? No sense getting it soaked.'

He faced her, holding his arms out from his sides, dirty palms upwards. Susan undid the buttons on his safari jacket, revealing a brown, muscular chest. When she had undone the last button, he turned his back and she drew the jacket from his shoulders and down over his arms.

He wore no vest and his back muscles rippled as he flexed his shoulders, then began to roll the spare wheel towards the hub. Susan smoothed the jacket and held it over one arm. Greg paused for a moment and glanced at the onlookers, then he beckoned Susan to come closer. He bent his head near hers and said quietly, 'Look after the jacket. There's quite a bit of cash in my wallet.'

She nodded and held his jacket tightly to herself.

Greg knelt and began fitting the spare to the hub, then he rolled the wheel nuts on by hand and reached for the four-ended wheel brace. A tiny urchin in a white vest and blue cotton shorts dropped to his knees and shuffled close to Greg and said, 'Let me do it, please?'

Greg nodded, then said, 'O.K., start turning.'

He handed the wheel brace to the boy, who carefully fitted the wrench end over one of the nuts and quite professionally began to spin the nut on to the bolt.

Susan found the sight of Greg's bare back oddly stimulating. She guessed he would be in his mid-thirties and he had obviously kept himself in excellent physical shape. He was muscular and sinewy, there was no flab anywhere on his frame and his stomach was hard and flat.

The boy had fitted on the last nut and twirled it with the wheel wrench as tightly as he could. Greg knelt beside him and took the tool, tightening each nut to its limit. Everything he did seemed quite effortless. Only a few trickles of sweat running down his back and chest, and his beaded brow, showed how even the smallest exertion in the Singapore heat resulted in instant perspiration. He reached for the chrome hubcap to clap it over the wheel, and the boy begged, 'Let me do, please!'

Greg said, 'O.K.—but you'll have to give it a hard knock to lock it in place.'

The boy nodded and carefully placed the hubcap in position, then hit it a few times with his palms. But he didn't have enough strength to force it on properly.

Greg could have knocked it on with one smack of his fist, but he didn't. Instead, he handed the boy the wheel brace, with its rubber end outwards. 'Here, use this,' he said. 'That's what it's for.'

The boy took the brace and began jabbing at the cap with the rubber end. He almost had it locked in position when his forearm slipped along the chisel edge of the brace used for prising off hubcaps, and he gave a squeal of pain as blood sprang from the long graze on his thin brown arm.

Greg quickly slapped the hubcap into place with his palm, then carefully took the lad by the arm and drew him up to a standing position.

'Poor little guy,' he said. 'You were trying too hard.' He held the boy's arm gently and studied the wound. It wasn't very deep, but there was a lot of blood. Tears welled up in the boy's eyes as he stared at his wound.

Greg said to Susan, 'Do you carry a first aid kit in the bus? I can clean this up and put something on it.'

She nodded. 'Yes. I'll get it.'

The jack was still in position, blocking the near-side door, so with Greg's safari jacket over her arm she squeezed through the onlookers and went round to the driver's side, opened the door and got in. She laid the jacket over the back of the seat while she reached over to the glove compartment on the passenger's side where the first aid kit was kept. It was in quite a heavy metal box and she needed both hands to carry it.

She scrambled out of the bus with the box and forced the door shut with her shoulder, then she hurried round to the other side and held the box out to Greg.

'You take this,' she said. 'I'll fix his arm.'

He took the box and said, 'No, I'll do it. This is man's work.' The boy gave a small smile.

Susan ground her teeth silently as Greg opened the box. To herself she muttered, 'Chauvinist pig!'

He took out some cotton wool and Aquaflavin, then he smiled at the boy and said, 'This won't hurt.' He poured antiseptic on the cotton wool and the boy winced when Greg applied it gently to the wound. He chatted to the boy as he worked until finally the bleeding stopped and he took a bandage from the box and tied it round the boy's thin forearm. Then he fished in his pants pocket and brought out some coins.

'Here's your pay,' he said. 'Right?'

The boy grinned and the last of his tears disappeared.

Greg patted his shoulder again and the boy fell back into the crowd, a few fellow urchins crowding round him to see how much money he had been given.

Greg picked up the first aid box and closed it, then looked at Susan. 'That's my Boy Scout deed for the day. So, if you'll put this box back I'll put the flat and the gear inside and we can get moving.'

Susan took the heavy first aid box from him as Greg quickly released the jack and began to load the wheel through the rear door. To keep out of his way, she walked round to the driver's side of the bus and opened the door and got in, then leaned across and replaced the box in the glove compartment. Then she got out again and walked round to where Greg had finished loading the wheel-changing equipment.

He straightened up, his bare brown torso glistening, and he flashed a crooked grin at her. 'O.K.,' he said, 'I'll have my jacket.'

Susan's hand flew to her mouth. As she had got into the driver's seat she hadn't noticed his jacket lying over the back of the seat where she'd left it.

'Oh, my God!' she cried, and Greg frowned slightly.

She dived in the rear door of the bus, hoping his

jacket had merely slipped over the back of the seat into the passenger compartment. But it wasn't there. Neither was it on the floor between the two front seats. A couple of quick glances were enough to tell her it wasn't anywhere. She got out of the bus and stared at Greg, who had been watching her as she frantically searched in the front and rear.

He looked at her, his brows knitting. But he didn't say anything, just rubbed his grimy hands together and eyed her coolly.

Susan felt like crying out with rage, frustration and humiliation. What a colossal idiot she'd been!

'I—I—it must have been stolen,' she groaned. 'God, I'm *sorry*!' Her eyes darted desperately around the onlookers. 'Maybe we can find who took it,' she said with faint hope. 'I—I'll ask some of these people if they saw it being taken.'

But remarkably, the crowd of onlookers instantly dispersed. Suddenly there was nobody near the bus except herself and Greg. And Greg was looking very grim.

Susan slapped herself furiously on the cheek, enraged at herself for her stupidity.

'I—I don't know *what* to say. How—how much money was in the jacket?'

'About five hundred dollars,' he said shortly.

'Singapore or American dollars?'

'American,' he said. 'In currency. I gave all my Singapore money to the boy.'

'Oh, lord!' Susan moaned. That was over a thousand Singapore dollars in his jacket—getting close to her month's salary without allowances.

'I'm so *sorry*!' she said helplessly. 'You did tell me there was money in it. I feel so stupid.'

He shrugged. 'Well, you said it.'

Her colour deepened. 'I really am sorry. But I— I'll replace the money for you. The company won't meet the loss—it says on the tickets that they're not responsible for valuables or money passengers leave in the buses.'

'*I* wasn't the one who left it in the bus,' he said coldly. 'You did.'

'I know, I know! That's why I'll make it good. It's too late for me to go to the bank today, they're closed. But I'll draw the money tomorrow and bring it round to your hotel.'

'Forget it,' he said briefly. 'I guess I can take a five hundred buck loss easier than you can. I'll write it off to experience.'

'No,' she said positively, 'I intend to repay you. That's quite definite.'

His jaw tightened. 'And it's equally definite that I won't take it. So let's get into the bus and get back to my hotel—that's if you think your goddam bus can make it without something else going wrong.'

His brow was black as he scowled angrily at her as she faced him, her body quivering.

'There's nothing wrong with our buses,' she said shortly. 'We—I—just had bad luck today.'

'O.K., forget it. Let's get in and get back so I can clean up. I sure won't forget my trip with Tiger Tours.'

Susan stamped her foot in exasperation. 'Don't blame the company! I'm the one to blame. And

I've apologised and said I'll make good the money. What more can I do?'

He looked at her bright pink face and snapping blue eyes as she stood, trembling with suppressed anger, glaring up at him.

'Well,' he growled, 'I think we should have a quiet cup of coffee somewhere until you recover your—equilibrium. So let's go find a coffee shop.'

'No, thank you!' she snapped. 'I—I'm too upset.'

'You sure are,' he agreed, surveying her quivering figure. 'I think you better let me drive us back. You don't look like you're fit to drive right now.'

Susan stamped her foot again. 'I'm perfectly all right! Anyway, only company personnel can drive company transport. So if you'd like to get in, I'll take you back.'

He shook his head. 'I'm not riding with you while you're all worked up. Let's have a drink until you cool down.'

'I'm not worked up!' she snapped, banging the door of the bus furiously. 'And anyway, we can't go for a drink with you half-naked.'

He nodded. 'Then let's just sit in the bus for a while till you get a grip on yourself. Then we'll go.'

Susan drew a deep quivering breath, then stalked round the front of the bus to the driver's side. But when she opened the driver's door, Greg was already in the driver's seat, looking at her. He had hurried round and jumped in the passenger door, then slid across into her seat.

Susan held the driver's door open and glared up at him.

'Would you kindly get out of my seat!' she snapped. 'You can't drive anyway—I've got the keys.'

He nodded. 'I know. But while I'm in the driver's seat you're not going anywhere.'

Susan was almost crying with rage.

'I think you're an absolute pig!' she exploded. 'And if you don't get out of that seat I—I'll——'

'You'll do what?' he enquired, his eyes cold.

'I'll find a policeman,' she cried. 'I'll report you. For—for obstruction—for—for something——'

He scowled at her. 'Get in and sit down. You can drive in a little while. But you've got to lose some of that steam first. You're all burned up.'

Susan drew a deep quivering breath. Then she said, slowly and evenly, 'You are the most infuriatingly arrogant man I've ever met. I didn't like you from the moment I met you. You're an overbearing pig and you think it's fun to throw your weight around, with someone weaker than you. You know I can't *force* you out of the seat, so you're just taking advantage of that fact. I *despise* men like you. You're a—a coward!'

She spat the word out and Greg's jaw tightened and he hunched his shoulders like a fullback. He swung himself down from the seat on to the road and she jumped back hastily as he stood menacingly over her, his face dark.

'If you were a man,' he growled, 'I'd break your prissy neck. So who's taking advantage of their sex now?'

She tossed her head. 'I'm not afraid of you!' she retorted, but at the same time she edged back out of his reach. 'But it wouldn't surprise me if you were to hit a woman!'

Greg slammed a clenched fist into his palm. He glared at her, then said vehemently, 'Why don't you take your goddam bus and drive it into the nearest light pole—which is what you'll probably do, given your general incompetence so far!'

'Oh!' Susan cried, launching herself towards him and raising her hands and furiously pummelling his hard brown chest. 'I—I——'

He grasped both her wrists with one strong hand and raised an admonishing finger with the other. Almost instantly, a small crowd of onlookers gathered again to watch the white man and the blonde girl having a fight. In the distance, Greg saw two white-uniformed Chinese policemen moving towards the disturbance.

'Relax,' he growled, 'or you'll have the cops on us. So take your bus—I'll find my own way back to the hotel.'

He released her hands and she rubbed her wrists furiously. Then he strode off, pushing his way through the bystanders.

'Hey!' she cried out after him. 'You haven't any money! I——'

He turned his head and snapped over his shoulder, 'I've got money at the hotel. A taxi will trust me that far.' He glared at her and stalked off through the crowd.

Susan put her hands on her hips as she watched his tall muscular frame shoulder its way through the teeming throng. His bare bronzed back silently reproached her until he swung stiffly round a corner and she lost sight of him.

Well, she thought bitterly, still fuming at his arrogance, there goes a highly dissatisfied customer. I'll be lucky if he doesn't contact the office and scream blue murder!

CHAPTER TWO

DRIVING back to Tiger Tours base at Paya Lebar, Susan was seething over her experience with Greg McKenzie. She told herself he was easily the most stubborn, infuriatingly arrogant man she'd ever met. He was also a sullen, bad-tempered pig, and during the whole afternoon he had only smiled about twice—once at her, after he had eaten his lunch, and a couple of times at the little Chinese boy who had hurt his arm. These were the only traces of humanity he had shown. He was just one of those people it was impossible to please.

Nevertheless, it hurt her professional pride to end a tour with a dissatisfied client. She had always been proud of her ability to get along with every kind of tourist—no matter how mean or nasty they might be. And in three years she had encountered some very unpleasant ones indeed.

Not that Greg McKenzie had been actually unpleasant—just boorish, sarcastic, overbearing, irritatingly superior—and generally infuriating!

Then, as she began to simmer down on the drive back to base, she grudgingly admitted that perhaps she hadn't been her even-tempered self that afternoon. She didn't like doing city tours anyway— they were completely different from the long, leisurely trips up country where everybody was relaxed. City tourists were mostly just filling in time, as Greg McKenzie had been doing. And like him, they were often critical of the city's lack of really interesting things to see.

Then too, she had received practically no warning that she was needed to take the tour out. She had had to drive from her apartment to the base, pick up the minibus and drive to the Mandarin—all within an hour. She hadn't even had time to change into her uniform. Then the rotten downpour had delayed her, trapping her in the bus outside the Mandarin for an hour. Then her other two clients had cancelled—so all she'd been doing for the company was losing money as she drove Greg McKenzie around.

Not that he had appreciated it, she thought bitterly. Then, as she neared the base, she remembered that she *had* lost his jacket. Which was going to cost her five hundred dollars, she reflected grimly.

She wasn't in a good mood as she swung the bus into Tiger Tours' sprawling main base. She would have to report her disastrous tour to David—for Greg McKenzie might very well lodge a complaint. But she would tell David she planned to make good the money tomorrow.

She drove the bus into the garage, then went to the chief mechanic's office and reported the flat tyre and also the ignition problem after the rain. Methodically, she also reported that the first aid kit had been used and should be checked. Then she walked across the asphalt to the briefing lounge where the tour conductors, guides and drivers waited before assignments.

It was a large, well-equipped room with a canteen serving drinks and snacks, but no alcohol. It had a number of comfortable lounges and chairs and there was a variety of recreational equipment with which the staff could amuse themselves before, after or between assignments.

Susan went to the canteen counter and ordered a Coca-Cola which was served by a smiling Chinese girl. As Susan left the counter, a stocky, brown-faced Malay in his early forties crossed to greet her.

'*Selamat*, Susan,' he said with a slight bow, and she returned his salam with a smile.

'Hello, Munir,' she said. 'I didn't expect to see you around today. Aren't you taking my tour out on Wednesday?'

He nodded and said in excellent English, 'Yes, I am off duty today and tomorrow. But I came in to collect my hard-earned salary. My wife is waiting to spend it at the expensive Singapore markets.'

Susan smiled. Munir, whose full name was Ahmad Munir bin Abraham, was a Malaysian citizen, although he was forced to live with his family in Singapore, where he was based. Like most Malays, he considered Singapore hideously expensive, which it was, compared with Malaya.

He was Tiger Tours' most senior driver, or coach captain, and Susan had done many tours with him. Traditionally, English people and the Malays got along well together. Both races tended to be reserved and respect the private feelings of others. But Susan had developed a warmer relationship with Munir than with any of the other drivers—

Chinese, Indian or Malay.

Munir pressed his hands together in a slightly Indian gesture of deference. 'And why are you here today? You should also be off duty, for you will be going with me on Wednesday.'

Susan sipped her Coke and said, 'David asked me to come in and do a city tour this afternoon. So many drivers are sick, he was very short-handed.'

Munir nodded. 'It's this terrible city water,' he said gravely. 'At home we drink only the purest rainwater caught in gourds.'

Susan smiled. Munir's love of his native *kampong* up north, near Ipoh, was well known. One day, when he had saved enough money, he planned to go back there.

She put down her glass. 'Well, I must go and see David. He's supposed to be taking me out tonight. Not that I feel much like it, I've had a terrible day.'

Munir nodded sympathetically. 'Those day tourists! I would not like to be driving the mini-buses again. Worse than being a taxi driver.'

Susan said goodbye and walked out of the lounge and along a covered verandah to the main offices.

She went into the big general office where about twenty clerks, mainly young Chinese girls, worked energetically in a clamour of chatter. At one end of the long room were the two executive offices, both identical in size, one for David, the General Manager, and one for K. Koh, the Managing Director.

Although David and Mr Koh had put similar amounts of money into Tiger Tours when they founded it, the business had been registered in Kuala Lumpur as a Malaysian company and under that country's laws, Europeans could only own forty-nine per cent of any business. So although David and K.K. were theoretically equal shareholders, K.K. had the majority say. But he left most of the decisions about Tiger Tours to David, for K.K. also had a thriving legal practice and didn't spend a lot of time at the tours offices.

Susan strolled through the general office until she reached David's secretary, a slim Eurasian girl called Helen Goh whose desk was just outside David's door. They greeted each other and Helen said David had someone with him, but he shouldn't be long. Then she lowered her sleek dark head conspiratorially and said, 'Tanya is with him. But I think she's only killing time. Mr Koh is due in any minute for a discussion with David, so naturally Tanya is hanging around.'

She smiled mischievously. She didn't like Tanya much, but she liked Susan.

Susan said, 'Well, if she's only killing time, I suppose I can go in and talk to him. David might welcome the interruption. I won't hold him up for long—I just want to report on my tour and cancel a date I had with him for tonight.'

Helen picked up her intercom phone. 'I'll tell him you're here.'

After Helen had announced her, Susan walked to David's door and pushed it open. He had already risen from behind his desk and he crossed to greet her, giving her hand a small squeeze.

Tanya, who was sprawled gracefully in the visitors' chair, didn't get up, but lay back and surveyed Susan languorously. As usual, she was strikingly dressed. She wore a tight-fitting Chinese *cheongsam* in pale blue silk with a silver dragon motif curling from the back around her hip to the hem at the front. The dress, which came to just below her knees, was slit thigh-high on both sides and her legs were crossed, displaying soft brown thighs and long shapely legs. Her sleek black hair hung in a coil over one shoulder.

She glanced at Susan, in her crumpled skirt and blouse, her blonde hair still slightly damp from her afternoon in the heat. Under Tanya's scrutiny, Susan felt a mess. Actually, she often felt like that in Tanya's presence, for Tanya had the attractive Eurasian girl's ability to wear any kind of clothes, Eastern or Western, and always look cool and exotic.

Tanya's mother had been half Chinese and her father a White Russian, but her Chinese ancestry wasn't especially pronounced. It showed mainly in her eyes, which were slightly almond-shaped, but no more so than many people from Southern Europe. She had been born in Hong Kong but had travelled a lot and spoke several languages, all excellently, like her English.

Tanya completed her cool, almost insolent survey of Susan, then said, 'Hello, Suzy. You look like you've had a bad day with the peasants.'

David frowned. He didn't like clients being called peasants. Susan gritted her teeth. She hated being called Suzy—and Tanya knew it. She nodded curtly to Tanya and said hello to David.

He held out the other visitors' chair for her and she perched on it, smoothing her rumpled skirt.

He said in his clipped tones, 'You do look as if you've had a bad day, Susan. The tour wasn't much fun, eh? Sorry to have asked you to take it, but I was at my wits' end.'

Susan shrugged. 'No, it wasn't much fun. And I only had one passenger, an objectionable American. And the bus wouldn't start after the rain. And we had a flat tyre.'

David clicked his tongue, his ruddy face sympathetic. He was dressed in tailored khaki shorts and long brown socks with an open-necked khaki shirt with two breast pockets, military style. His sleeves were neatly rolled to just above the elbows, and the colour of his arms, like that of his face and neck, was light red. In spite of his years in the tropics he had never tanned. He had short reddish hair and greeny blue eyes that looked at Susan with affection.

'Tell me about it,' he said sympathetically, perching on the end of his desk, facing the two girls.

Tanya put one hand to her mouth and yawned delicately. Susan tightened her lips, then said to David, 'I already have. Except that this American—Greg McKenzie was his name—was a rude, arrogant pig. He actually thought he could drive the bus better than I could!'

David clicked his tongue again and Susan tersely continued to tell him what she thought of Greg McKenzie.

Then she added, 'But to cap it all, I lost his jacket with a lot of money in it. Or anyway, his jacket was stolen—but it was my fault.'

David asked what exactly had happened and she told him, ending with Greg's bare-chested stalking away and leaving her.

She said forlornly, 'I really shouldn't have fought with him. But I told him I'd replace his money—which I will tomorrow. So what more could I do?'

David nodded. 'Well, I know you're not noted for being unpleasant to clients—quite the reverse. So I imagine he must have been rather an impossible chap.'

'Impossible is the word,' Susan said feelingly.

David shrugged. 'He won't be a satisfied customer, that's certain. But I suppose we can't win them all. I'm sure you handled him as best you could.'

Tanya yawned slightly, then murmured, 'I never have any trouble with clients. Not the males anyway.'

'You might have had trouble with this one,' Susan said grimly. 'He *was* impossible!'

Tanya got to her feet and sauntered towards the door. 'I'd have let him drive the bus,' she said. 'Who cares?'

David frowned. 'I do,' he said. 'The company does. Susan was perfectly——'

There was a sharp tap on the door, then it opened and a small, dapper Chinese man came in. He was immaculately dressed in a light blue silk suit with a pale blue shirt and a blue and silver striped tie. His blue-tone leather shoes shone like his sleek black hair, which was brushed straight back, close to his head. He had a sharp-featured, olive-skinned face with penetrating black eyes that surveyed them unblinkingly.

David said easily, 'Hello, K.K.'

Mr Koh nodded. Behind his back he was referred to by the staff as K.K. His intimates, like David and Tanya, called him K.K. to his face. To everyone else he was Mr Koh. Nobody, not even David, knew what the first K in his name stood for. Although he was close to fifty, K.K. could easily have passed for forty or younger.

He moved briskly into the room, smacking his palm with a copy of the afternoon newspaper. He nodded politely to Susan and more warmly to Tanya, then said, 'Excuse me, ladies. I have something important to show David.'

Susan made to leave, but K.K. waved her to stay. 'I won't be long,' he said in his excellent, Oxford-educated English. He opened the newspaper and folded it back to page three, then said to David, 'Here is someone we should contact very urgently. This could be big business for us.'

David took the paper and began reading the item K.K. had pointed out. As David read, K.K. walked over to Tanya and said he was looking forward to seeing her at the cocktail party he was giving at his home tomorrow night. His manner to Tanya was formal, but Tanya didn't try to hide the slightly possessive look in her eye as she said she would be there and was sure she would enjoy it.

While David read, K.K. said to Susan, 'And I hope you will be present too. No doubt you will be coming with David?'

Susan nodded her thanks. K.K.'s cocktail parties were almost compulsory for senior staff like her. He held them about four times a year and they were very lavish. More like buffet dinners than cocktail parties. Most of the guests were from the travel industry—airline executives, hotel management, travel agents, government people from the Singapore Tourist Promotion Board. In fact, anyone whose goodwill could be useful to Tiger Tours, including visiting dignitaries from Malaysia who happened to be in Singapore.

There was a sudden strangled cry from David and they all looked at him.

He clapped a hand to his brow and said to Susan, 'What was the name of your American?'

Susan said, puzzled, 'McKenzie—Greg McKenzie.'

David said faintly, 'From Los Angeles?'

Susan nodded. David muttered, 'Oh, my God!'

K.K. said sharply, 'What's the matter, David? What's this about?'

David thrust the folded paper at Susan and stabbed at a picture with his finger. 'Is that your American—the one between the two Tourist Board executives?'

Susan took the paper and glanced at the picture. It certainly was Greg. He towered over the two Chinese on either side of him. He was wearing the same safari suit he had worn on the tour with her.

David waved an arm at her. 'Read it!' he said sharply.

Susan glanced at the caption, which read, 'Mr

Greg McKenzie, President of Trans Asia Tours,
Los Angeles, was guest of honour at a reception
this morning at the Singapore Tourist Promotion
Board's offices. He was received by the Chairman
of the Board and the Tourism Minister.'

Slowly, Susan raised her eyes to David. He said
tersely, 'Read the story—that'll tell you everything.'

Quickly Susan scanned the report with the picture.

It said that Mr McKenzie was owner of one of
the largest tour operations on the U.S. West Coast.
His company specialised in tours of Asia, although
they hadn't yet run tours to Singapore or Malaysia.
Mr McKenzie was visiting the two countries to
assess their potential for being included in some of
his tours. In Singapore and Malaysia he was
regarded as a VIP by the tourist industry—and the
government.

That was enough for Susan, although there was
more about Greg's background and how he had
started as a truck driver, graduated to driving
tourist coaches, then founded his own travel company which finally specialised in Asian tours. His
company's turnover was many millions of dollars
and fifteen per cent of all American tourists who
visited Taiwan, for example, arrived on one of his
tours. The report also gave his age as thirty-six.

K.K. had been waiting impatiently while Susan
read the report. Finally he said, his voice smooth
but steely, 'Would someone tell me what's going
on?'

Tanya said lightly, 'Nothing really. Greg

McKenzie was on our city tour this afternoon—driven by Susan. They had a small argument and Mr McKenzie lost his shirt—and his money—then finally took a taxi back to his hotel rather than enjoy our tour any longer.'

K.K.'s smooth brows knitted. He said, 'Susan, would you kindly tell me all about this—in your own words.'

Haltingly, Susan repeated the whole story, and when she was finished, K.K. said, 'Well, that was really rather clever, Susan. I came in to tell David that we should at all costs make contact with Mr McKenzie and invite him to my party tomorrow night. I planned to call on him myself, offer him courtesy transport—a limousine, a driver, an escort—anything we could do for him. In other words, treat him like the VIP he is. And now I find he's already had an example of our service—and what an example!' He shook his sleek head. 'Oh, jolly good—one up for Tiger Tours!'

He looked at Susan, his face wrinkled in an expression of disgust and annoyance.

'It's not fair!' Susan burst out. 'I had no idea he was in the travel business, and a VIP. I asked him what he did and he said he was an exporter.'

'Yes,' said K.K., 'he exports people—tourists. And does Tiger Tours ever need tourists!'

David said, 'I gather from the newspaper report that McKenzie always vets any new countries personally, tries out all the tourist services and hotels. Presumably he does this incognito, for he'd know that once the travel industry knew who he was, he'd get special VIP treatment. I don't suppose you can blame him for operating that way.'

Susan said defensively, 'I still think he was a rat, not telling me who he was. Or at least that he was in travel. Not that it makes any difference—he was still objectionable!'

K.K. said, 'But however objectionable he might have been, you would have been nicer to him had you known who he was and how valuable he could be to us?'

'Yes, I suppose I would,' Susan said shortly.

Tanya drawled, 'I certainly would—have been nice to him. I hope I still get the chance.'

K.K. glanced at her speculatively. 'You might,' he said. 'David and I will try and make contact with Mr McKenzie tonight. Perhaps you will join us, Tanya, and we may be able to repair some of the damage Susan has done.'

Tanya smiled and David said, 'We'll have to pass up our dinner date tonight, Susan. It's very important that we get on side with McKenzie.'

Susan tossed her head. 'I came in to ask if we could skip dinner tonight. I'm too upset. So, if you'll please excuse me.'

With her head high she strode stiffly towards the door.

Tanya called out sweetly, 'We'll remember you to Greg McKenzie tonight, Suzy.'

K.K. said quickly, 'No, we won't do that. I doubt if Mr McKenzie will forget Susan.'

CHAPTER THREE

SUSAN spent a thoroughly miserable night in her small modern apartment in Tanglin. She didn't feel like eating, but drank several cups of coffee as she wandered from the living room to the bedroom, then into her small kitchen. The apartment had a tiny verandah, but it was still hot outside and she kept the sliding doors tightly closed to preserve the air-conditioning that made tropical living bearable.

The air-conditioning in her apartment was very efficient. She had put on a light wool dressing gown after she had come home and pulled off her crumpled clothes, then had a shower to cool down.

After her third cup of coffee she dug out her bank book, and groaned when she saw that after she had paid Greg McKenzie his five hundred dollars she would have less than that amount left in her account. Which would represent her total savings after three years' hard work in Singapore.

Few Europeans ever saved much in the East. For although they mostly received higher salaries than Asians—even when doing the same job—there was a higher standard of living that Europeans were almost forced to live up to.

And, Susan reflected grimly, she could well be in danger of losing her job.

She had no illusions about what K.K. thought about her—especially after her big gaffe today.

K.K. was normally fairly easy-going. But one thing that upset him was the possibility of losing money—or missing out on a profitable deal. And Susan knew she had been the cause of making the Very Important Mr McKenzie very anti-Tiger Tours.

She put her bankbook into the blue handbag she would take with her tomorrow morning, and thought about Greg McKenzie and his unpardonable behaviour by coming on her tour under false pretences. She could appreciate what David had said about McKenzie not wanting to reveal his identity so he could try out the tour in the guise of a regular tourist. But it was still a dirty trick—and she'd tell him so when she saw him tomorrow morning and gave him his money back.

Then she thought she had better not tell him what she thought of him. She had already done that—very bluntly. She couldn't afford—for David and the company's sake—to antagonise him further and do more damage. Thinking about how restrained she would have to be, she ground her teeth. She would prefer to stalk coldly up to him at the Mandarin and throw the five hundred dollars at his feet. Then perhaps spit in his eye as he knelt to pick it up!

But she knew she would have to deny herself that pleasure. And perhaps even humble herself a little to try to undo some of the harm she had caused.

Oh, to hell with him, she thought. It hadn't been her fault. Not all her fault anyway. He *had* been a pig—arrogant, superior and boorish. And hard to get on with. But still, he had been rather a nice-looking pig. More like a boar. Very definitely more like a boar, she thought as she recalled his muscular brown torso when he had worked shirtless changing the wheel.

He did look like a truck driver, she mused, undoing her dressing gown which was beginning to make her feel hot. An intelligent truck driver, but nevertheless a very physical kind of male. Definitely physical, she thought, flapping the lapels of her gown to cool herself. She imagined he had plenty of girls—but why shouldn't he, if he wasn't married?

She wondered why he hadn't married. He must have had plenty of opportunities. Then she realised most girls probably had more sense. Not too many girls these days were prepared to be doormats—which would be essential for anyone who wanted to be Greg McKenzie's wife!

She got up and slipped off her dressing gown and tossed it over a chair. Then, clad only in brief panties, she went into the bathroom and contemplated taking another shower. The apartment now seemed warm, although the air-conditioning was full on.

She turned on the shower taps, then glanced at herself in the bathroom mirror.

She had combed her blonde hair loose and although she wore no make-up, her peaches and cream complexion didn't really need any. She was the traditional English Rose in colouring, but she had tanned herself carefully since she had been in the East and her skin had a golden glow. A lighter strip across her rounded bosom showed she had never sunbathed topless.

She thought her figure looked rather good, with high firm breasts, narrow waist and curving hips leading to long, tapering legs which looked very shapely as she stood on tiptoe in front of the mirror. She had swum once at a hotel pool when Tanya had been one of the party and they had both worn bikinis. Susan thought her figure was every bit as good as Tanya's, although she had to admit it was Tanya in a bikini who had drawn most of the male eyes.

The difference between them was that Tanya looked—sexy. Even fully-clothed, Tanya looked very exciting. Susan felt that was not a description that could be applied to herself. Although David seemed to think she was exciting enough, or anyway, he told her she was. He would have liked her to be more sexy—but something always held her back. She didn't want to throw herself away on any man because she was in the exotic East. One day she would get married, although David was the only man who had asked her, and the prospect of marriage to David wasn't especially exciting.

She spent a disturbed night, turning over in her mind what she would say to Greg McKenzie next morning when she gave him his money. She decided finally on a very dignified approach. She would be formal and polite—and even make some kind of apology for their disastrous tour. She thought that would be sufficiently generous on her part.

Next morning she dressed carefully in a pale blue

shirt-dress in pure silk. It had accentuated shoulders and a narrow skirt with a white tie belt. She wore white shoes and carried her blue handbag.

Then she visited the Hong Kong and Shanghai Bank and drew the money, then drove to the Mandarin Hotel, only to find that Mr McKenzie wasn't in. The desk clerk said he didn't know when he would be back, although he usually returned at lunchtime to collect his messages. Susan resigned herself to waiting and had morning tea to fill in time. Then, towards noon, she glanced up from where she had seated herself in the lobby and saw Tanya entering the hotel.

Tanya wore a striking slip of a dress in iridescent pink silk. It was shirred wide across padded shoulders, slashed to the fitted waist and accented with a sash of neon red silk which matched the lining on her tuxedo-style collar. The glowing dress was split high in front to reveal Tanya's long brown legs as she walked across the lobby. She looked very exotic and drew the eyes of several waiting males—who quickly glanced away when they saw the powerful build of her escort.

Susan's heart sank when she saw that the man with Tanya was Greg, who was wearing light grey slacks and an open-necked sports shirt. Tanya was holding his arm familiarly, and Susan reflected bitterly that she hadn't wasted any time giving Greg the VIP treatment.

Susan had dressed very carefully for her visit to Greg and she had done her hair in a soft bouffant style that delicately framed her oval face. But contrasted with Tanya's vivid dress and sleek black hair, Susan felt pale and insipid.

She got to her feet as they walked towards the desk, laughing and chatting. For a moment she was tempted to melt back into her seat—they'd probably never notice her—but Tanya spotted her almost at once and waved, then possessively steered Greg towards her.

'Hello, Suzy!' Tanya called as they drew closer. 'Fancy meeting you here.'

Greg said evenly, 'Hello, Miss York. Are you here to escort another tour?'

Susan flushed. 'No—I—I came to see you.'

He raised one eyebrow. 'Oh? O.K., we can fix that. Let me check the desk for messages and maybe return a couple of phone calls, then I'll be all yours.' He glanced at Tanya and said, 'That's if Tanya's through with me?'

Tanya pouted. 'I thought we might have lunch, Greg, then I could show you more of the island.'

He shook his head. 'I'm afraid I'm booked for lunch—business. Anyway, you've shown me about all I want to see today.'

Tanya smiled. 'And don't forget what I showed you last night.' She looked at Susan. 'We really saw the night life of Singapore.'

Greg nodded. 'We sure did. I enjoyed your company. You know this town pretty well.'

Tanya smiled, deliberately arch, 'It was my pleasure entirely.'

Greg said, 'Anyway, I'll see you this evening at K.K.'s party. But right now, if you'll excuse me, I must collect my messages.'

Tanya held out her hand and Greg took it and

squeezed it briefly. To Susan he said, 'If you'll hang on, I'll be through soon.' He turned and strode towards the desk.

Tanya followed him with her eyes, then she wrenched them back to Susan. 'What a delightful hunk of man—and so sexy too!' She fluttered her eyelashes in mock innocence.

Susan said evenly, 'He's quite attractive.'

Tanya said, 'Attractive? I'll say. And *very* commanding. I didn't get home until after four this morning. He took me up to his suite—for a nightcap. Then afterwards, he was very gentlemanly and escorted me back to K.K.'s car.'

Susan's lips tightened. 'I'm sure all the hotel staff knew you were here last night. I mean, you do visit the suites quite often.'

Tanya smiled. 'Tut, tut—bitchy little Suzy! It doesn't become your sweet English nature. And that dress you're wearing doesn't become you much either,' she added tartly.

Susan squared her shoulders. 'Goodbye, Tanya. I've got business with Mr McKenzie.' She began to walk stiffly away.

'Bye-bye,' Tanya called. 'See you tonight at K.K.'s. Oh, and don't accept the first proposition Greg makes, when you're talking business.'

Susan tried to ignore her trilling laugh as she walked towards the desk and waited a few feet from Greg while he riffled through his messages.

He glanced up and saw her and frowned abstractedly. He gave some instructions to the desk clerk, then tucked the messages in his pocket and walked over to her.

He glanced at his watch and said, 'I've got half an hour before lunch. How about we have a drink?'

Susan hesitated. She didn't really want to prolong the meeting, but she had planned to be as nice to him as she could. So she said all right, and he led her over to one of the tables near the hotel entrance where they could look out at the street.

A slim Chinese waiter appeared like a genie and placed canapés before them, then asked Greg for their order. Susan said she would have a mineral water and Greg asked for a beer.

Greg studied her as they waited for the drinks. His eyes roamed over her pale, composed face and he said, 'You look much cooler today. Your dress—the colour suits you—nice, icy blue.'

She felt her cheeks turning pink, but she forced a smile, then said, as lightly as she could, 'I gather Tanya's been showing you the sights.'

He nodded. 'Your Mr Koh—and your boyfriend, David Farrell—called to see me last night. Tanya was with them. We had drinks and a long talk, then they had to leave, so Tanya showed me the town.'

Susan lowered her eyes. 'You had quite a late night, I gather. Although you look quite fresh today.'

He grunted, but said nothing as the waiter glided up and placed their drinks before them.

He raised his glass. 'Good luck—or better luck today anyway. For us both,' he added.

They touched glasses and drank, then Susan said quickly, 'I've come to replace the money that was stolen.' She opened her bag and took out the notes. 'Here it is—five hundred American dollars.' She pushed the money across the table towards him.

He nodded, but didn't touch the money. 'You're very determined, aren't you? But as you may have realised, I'm just as determined. I said I didn't want to take the money from you.'

She shrugged. 'And I said I intended to pay it to you. So—here it is.' She looked at him challengingly, then dropped her eyes under his cold gaze. Quickly she forced a smile. 'We'd better not leave it on the table. The waiter would have a heart attack if he found such a big tip!'

Greg's cool expression relaxed—only slightly—then he said, 'Your K.K. insisted on replacing the money last night. And I accepted it. He seems like he can afford it. So I've got my money back—and I don't want it twice.' He pushed the bundle of notes towards her. 'So why don't you put that back in your bag and maybe buy yourself something you didn't plan to, now that you're richer than you thought you'd be?'

Susan bit her lip, then slowly picked up the money and replaced it in her bag.

'All right,' she said. 'Thank you.'

'And don't let K.K. take it out of your salary,' he added. 'He looks like a sharp man with a buck. But I told him I didn't want you to suffer over—my loss. I think he'll listen—he badly wants to do business with my company.'

She nodded. 'Yes. Everybody in the Singapore travel industry does. I didn't know you were so—so important.'

He shrugged. 'I try to make these trips incognito. But word gets around fast in the travel business. I couldn't get out of that government reception yesterday. It would have been bad policy for me to turn them down, for it's possible we may want to run tours to Singapore. But I would preferred to have poked around with nobody knowing who I was, or what I'm here for.'

'And why are you here?'

He settled himself comfortably in his padded chair. 'Well, Trans Asia Tours has to keep coming up with new places to go. Until now we've concentrated on Japan, Taiwan and the Philippines. But we've got to widen our programmes. That's why I'm here—surveying the potential.'

Susan nodded. 'I suppose you have to study a place carefully before you decide to run tours to it.'

'We sure give it a lot of thought. You never know how a new tour programme will sell. And even scheduling only one departure a week from L.A. could commit us over a year to spending—and maybe losing—a quarter of a million dollars. So that's why I go over the ground very carefully before deciding on creating a new tour.'

Susan forced a smile. 'And that's why you don't tell people who you are?'

He nodded. 'I try not to—for as long as I can. Although it costs me money that way, for you probably know I could get around the world practically free. The airlines, hotels, car rental companies—they all want business from us, which is why I get the VIP treatment. Regular travel agents get the same free facilities.'

Susan nodded. Tiger Tours had often hosted visiting travel agents on what were called familiarisation trips so they could personally experience the product they would sell in their home countries.

Greg sipped his beer, then said, 'As far as possible I like to sample what we're selling to our clients—by exposing myself to the same treatment and service the ordinary client will get. I can't base my decision on the special VIP treatment tour companies and hotels turn on for me.'

Susan said, 'So—how does Tiger Tours come out?' She grimaced. 'Yesterday was hardly a brilliant example of our service—which I assure you is really very good, most of the time.'

He nodded. 'I'm sure it is. Your K.K. and David seem good operators. Your bus was late—but that was the rain. As you said, it was an older bus, but it was clean. Then, even for only one passenger, you didn't cancel—a lot of companies would have. You explained that you weren't a regular city tour driver, but you knew your stuff—about Singapore, I mean. And most of the time you talked intelligently—and you drove quite well.'

She swallowed. 'But I managed to lose your jacket and money.'

'We all get the bad breaks. I got my money back, from Tiger Tours. Maybe I wouldn't have got it so readily if K.K. hadn't known who I am. But you intended to replace it out of your own pocket, even before you knew I was important businesswise. So—how can I knock that for looking after a client?'

Susan took a deep breath. 'So—maybe we're not too bad?' she asked hopefully.

He nodded. 'I'll tell you after I've been on one of your tours up into Malaysia. Tanya's told me more about them and I think maybe I'll try one—part of the way, anyway. She says she's taking the tour out tomorrow and I've tentatively arranged with K.K. to go on it.'

Susan's mouth dropped open. '*I'm* taking tomorrow's tour out! Tanya isn't scheduled to take hers until Friday. That's our roster.'

He raised his eyebrows. 'Yes, I thought you told me that yesterday. But I assumed you'd switched with Tanya. K.K. told me she was tomorrow's tour conductor.'

Susan gripped her glass so tightly she was surprised it didn't break.

Greg placed one hand over hers around the glass. 'Easy,' he said, 'you're starting to get burned up again.'

She relaxed her grip and forced a smile. 'I'm sorry. I—I'll sort it all out at the office. I feel fine.'

He glanced at her taut face and said, 'O.K., then how about having lunch with me?'

She stared at him. 'But you told Tanya you had a business lunch.'

He nodded. 'Yes—with you. You said you wanted to talk business.'

'Oh?' Susan sat up in her chair. 'But I've finished talking business. I only came to replace your money.'

'I know,' he said, 'and I'm glad our business talk is over. I get sick of working lunches on these trips—so how about we make it a personal one? Nobody trying to sell anybody anything?'

He looked at her gravely and she realised his hand was still round hers, which was holding her glass. She quickly slid her hand from under his.

'Thank you,' she said, colouring slightly. 'I'd be happy to have lunch with you.'

He nodded and signalled the waiter for the check. 'You know,' he said, 'you're a different person, when you're not driving a bus.'

She felt herself tensing slightly, resentment rising, then she forced it down and managed a smile. He was trying to be pleasant, so she wouldn't rise to his baiting.

'Thank you,' she said, 'and you're very different too—when you're not riding in a bus. I agree, you're not a very good tourist, are you?'

He put both hands over hers. 'No, but this time I'll try to be better company.'

She coloured and tried to draw her hand away, but he kept his hands firmly over hers. She studied his face, trying to see what he was thinking, but his dark eyes were fathomless.

She said, 'I'm sure you can be very good company, when you want to.'

Greg nodded as the waiter approached with the check. 'I want to,' he said. 'You'll be surprised how nice I can be.'

She bit off a retort and quickly lowered her eyes. She *would* be surprised if Greg McKenzie had a nice side. If he had, then he'd kept it well hidden—at least from her.

She glanced up and found he was studying her

closely. 'You don't believe me?' he said.

He lifted his hands from hers to pick up the check. He tossed down some notes and the waiter took them, bowed and glided away.

Greg said, 'We got off to a bad start. Things should improve, if you stop being so touchy.'

Susan's mouth dropped open. 'Me—touchy?' she choked. 'I—I——'

Words failed her as he got to his feet, then took her by the arm and raised her from her chair.

'Yes,' he said calmly. 'You've got to learn to control that temper. Otherwise we'll spend the whole lunch time quarrelling.'

She stared at him, then shook her head. 'You really are the most incredibly—arrogant man I've ever met!' She tried to shake off his arm as she stood looking up at his expressionless face.

Then suddenly he grinned, and it was the first time she had seen him display real amusement. He also looked rather nice when he smiled, and she was momentarily confused as he tightened his grip on her arm and guided her from the table.

'This could be a very militant lunch,' he murmured. 'Unless you'd like to agree to a truce for sixty minutes?'

She struggled to control herself as he led her towards the restaurant. 'All right,' she said tersely, 'a truce. For one hour.'

'Good,' he said. 'We might even become friendly.'

'We might,' she said shortly as she let him lead her across the lobby, 'if you'd stop trying to get the last word!'

'I'm rarely guilty of that,' he said calmly. 'That's one of your less endearing traits. You should learn to control it.'

She halted abruptly and shook his arm off as he paused beside her and looked at her coolly. She opened her mouth, but before she could speak he raised one hand, palm facing her, 'Truce,' he said, 'remember?'

She swallowed hard, then stalked ahead of him into the restaurant. If it hadn't been for the sake of David and the company she would have walked out of the hotel and left him standing.

She was furiously aware that if he needled her just once more she would choke on her food—or throw it at him, and to hell with his importance to Tiger Tours!

CHAPTER FOUR

BACK in her apartment after lunch Susan threw herself down on the bed, her mind in a whirl of confusion. She thought Greg McKenzie was really the most frustratingly unpredictable man!

During lunch he had been almost charming. He had been very attentive and never once said anything to annoy her. On the contrary, he had come close to apologising for his attitude on the tour yesterday. He had told her that assessing tours was always hard work and he rarely relaxed, for he committed everything he experienced to memory, then later he wrote up his findings.

'But you're seeing a different side of me now,' he said, 'because I'm relaxing.'

They lingered over coffee and he asked about her life. But at first Susan refused to be drawn, so he told her something about himself. He said his overseas trips were rarely much fun. It was hard slog all the way.

'And,' he added wryly, 'as I told you, I'm a lousy tourist. My ideal vacation is to get into my jeep and drive to the mountains where I camp for a week and mainly go fishing. I deal with people all the time, so on vacation I like to get away from them.'

After he had told her this, she felt she understood him better. He also told her something of his early life before he became a successful tour operator. How he had left college after graduating in Engineering—but engineering jobs had been scarce, so he started driving trucks. He had driven them in places as remote as the jungles of South America. Then he had begun driving tourist coaches—until finally, with slender capital, he had gone into business for himself, which developed eventually into Trans Asia Tours.

'So much for four hard years working for an Engineering degree.' He smiled wryly. 'It's the one skill I've never used.'

Then he asked her about herself, and she told him more about her life and childhood in Dorset. Compared with his, she felt her life had been mundane and boring, but he displayed a lot of interest in the trivia of her schooldays, her relationship with her father, and her first job in London with a travel agent, then her three years with Tiger Tours.

'I'm really not a very interesting person,' she concluded.

Greg shrugged. 'You've got guts,' he said, 'and people with guts are always interesting. There's not many of them around. And rarely so nicely packaged,' he added.

He had looked at her closely when he said this and she had been forced to drop her eyes quickly.

He had then told her he expected he would be seeing her at K.K.'s party that night. 'I hope I'll be able to relax tonight,' he said, 'if K.K. doesn't pin me down and give me the hard sell.'

As she lay thinking about Greg Susan remembered she had a bone to pick with K.K. But she thought she had better start with David, for all tour scheduling was handled by him, including the tour conductors' roster.

She phoned him at the office and came straight to the point.

'What's this about the roster being changed and me not taking out tomorrow's tour? I understand Tanya's taking it instead?'

David's voice was conciliatory. 'I'm sorry, Susan,' he said, 'but it was K.K.'s idea.' He hesitated, and Susan said coldly,

'Yes?'

'Well,' he went on, 'when we met Greg McKenzie last night, he and Tanya seemed to hit it off rather well. So K.K. more or less promoted the idea of Tanya taking the tour out, so she could—could——'

'Give Greg her personal attention?' Susan said sarcastically. 'Butter him up and make up for the bad time he had with me? Was that the idea?'

David's voice sounded lame. 'Well, something like that. I didn't agree with it—switching you for Tanya, I mean. But I had to go along with K.K. I mean, I could see the sense in it—after all, you and McKenzie didn't hit it off too well . . .' His voice tailed off.

Susan gripped the receiver. 'We got off on the wrong foot, Greg and I. But you may like to know that I've just had lunch with him, and he has no hard feelings about yesterday. In fact,' she added, 'we now get along quite well.'

'Oh?' his voice was nonplussed. 'Well, I don't think anything can be done about it now. Tanya's down for tomorrow's tour. But you can report for work as usual and we'll find something for you to fill in with until you take Friday's tour out.'

Susan said coldly, 'Don't you think it would have been the decent thing to have advised me I wasn't wanted tomorrow? I mean, did you plan to tell me when I reported with my suitcase all ready to go?'

He said weakly, 'No—no, I planned to phone you today. I—I——'

'You were putting it off,' she snorted. 'You couldn't face telling me, so you were procrastinating.'

Normally, Susan didn't use big words like procrastinating. She generally only used them when she wanted to make someone feel uncomfortable. And she badly wanted to make David feel uncomfortable.

He said placatingly, 'Look, how about if you forget about reporting tomorrow? Have an extra two days off and report on Friday. How does that sound?'

She said, tight-lipped, 'You're very generous. Thank you very much. And thank K.K. too. Greg McKenzie must really be important to K.K. if he gives someone two extra days off!'

David said, 'I hope you won't say anything—upsetting—to K.K. You will be coming with me to his party tonight?'

'I'll think about it,' she said coldly. 'I don't know which would annoy K.K. most—if I turned up, or if I didn't.'

She had slammed the phone down and gone into

the bathroom. Normally she would have started packing her case for her rostered tour tomorrow. K.K.'s parties usually went on until late, so she would have had little time to pack before her early start. But now she didn't need to pack.

She decided to use the unexpected free time by giving herself a manicure and facial. So she spent the afternoon pampering her face and body, ending with a relaxing soak in a fragrantly scented bath.

Then she spent a long time on her hair, trying it several ways before she decided on a soft, classical style.

At six o'clock David phoned. He was humble and conciliatory and he asked if he could pick her up at seven. She said she would be ready and he thanked her and rang off.

She got out her newest evening outfit. Apart from trying it on at the shop, then trying it again when she got home, she had never worn it.

She dressed, slipped on her shoes, applied the final touches to her hair, then studied herself in the full-length mirror.

She had put on a sleeveless jacket in lemon-coloured, cobwebby Chantilly lace with a moderately low-cut V-neck. It topped a flowing skirt in silky chiffon and had a large yellow rose at the waist. To complete the picture, she added crystal drop earrings. She thought she looked rather good and that the outfit had been worth its terrible price.

She got out her small yellow evening bag and sorted a few things into it, then put a romantic strings record on her stereo and sat down to await David's arrival.

But she didn't think about David. It was Greg who dominated her thoughts as she sat curled up on the sofa, the dreamy music creating a velvety background to the lush tropical night. She thought Greg was really rather a—a—she searched for the right word—a *memorable* man. Not the kind you forgot easily, with his unpredictable behaviour.

Certainly he had stayed in or near the forefront of her thoughts since she had met him. Although apart from taking her to lunch, he didn't seem especially interested in her.

But then he was a visiting businessman on a flying trip to the East, so he wanted female company. Not, she thought grimly, that he lacked it, with Tanya throwing herself at him! In his short stay here he was hardly likely to want to spend time chasing Susan when he only had to click his fingers to get the glamorous Tanya.

She thought about Tanya in his suite last night, and thinking about it destroyed the dreamy atmosphere created by the music. And now, on the tour starting tomorrow, Tanya would have him all to herself! He mightn't stay all the way with the tour, as he'd said, but tomorrow he would be alone with Tanya on their first overnight stop in Malacca.

Susan was glad when the bell rang and she let David in. He complimented her on her appearance and on her dress. She thought she must look pretty good, for David was moved out of his normal reticence and told her she looked like a film actress—and from David, there was no higher praise.

They drove in his Mercedes to K.K.'s sprawling,

luxury bungalow at Jurong. The house was Western style, but a mass of Chinese lanterns had been strung around the garden to create a festive, Oriental atmosphere. The delicate lantern light illuminated the manicured lawn around the big oval swimming pool and a yellow tropical moon was reflected in the sparkling water. Tables laden with food and drink had been set up at both ends of the pool, and discreet, white-jacketed Chinese waiters padded softly among the guests.

Susan wondered again why K.K. modestly described his functions as cocktail parties, for they were as lavish as any dinner. And although around seven was the starting time, they usually went on until one or two in the morning.

David was dressed in a white sharkskin dinner jacket and black pants. K.K., who greeted them on the patio, was identically dressed.

K.K. indicated he wanted David to stay at his side and welcome guests. To Susan he said, 'Sultan Khedar is over there with his son. Perhaps you could join them? I know young Khedar is anxious to see you.'

Susan nodded. Sultan Khedar was very important to Tiger Tours, for their tour route ran through the Northern Malay state of which he was the hereditary ruler. His son had earlier in the year graduated from Cambridge. His mother, the Sultan's second wife, was English, so the son was very Westernised. He had a number of advanced ideas, one being that the family home, Khedar Palace, should be opened up more to tourists. Through David, whom he regarded as a friend, the young heir three months ago began receiving a weekly group of Tiger Tour clients and accommodating them at the palace during one night of the Malaysian tour. The Sultan had given this his tacit approval, for he felt he had to permit his energetic and often impetuous son some scope to try out some of his modern ideas.

She made her way across the lawn, smiling at various guests, who were mostly men, and predominantly Chinese, but with a number of Europeans and Americans as well as a few Indians, Malays and assorted nationalities who made up Singapore's multi-ractial society. The men were quick to return Susan's smile, for as usual there was a shortage of females at the party. And there was an even greater shortage of attractive ones like Susan.

But Susan kept weaving through the beckoning guests until she reached the edge of the pool where Sultan Khedar was standing with his son and a red-faced, middle-aged grey-moustached Englishman who was holding a gin and tonic. The Sultan, and his son, both held glasses of orange juice.

All three men moved towards her when they saw her coming. 'Hello, Miss York,' the Sultan cried, extending one hand.

Susan touched his hand and made the slightest of curtsies. 'Good evening, Your Highness,' she said.

The Sultan, a stocky man in his late fifties, with close-cropped, iron grey hair, wore a simple brocaded white jacket and dark pants. Like his son, he was very Westernised.

He said, 'And my son, of course——' He gestured with one hand at the slim, olive-skinned young Malay, who smiled at her, relief flooding his handsome face at the arrival of someone around his own age.

'Hello, Susan,' he said, taking her hand and squeezing it. 'I'm very pleased to see you again.'

'Hello, Jimmy,' she said.

When she first met him, Susan hadn't been sure how to address him. She knew his full title comprised about fourteen separate Malay names. But at their first meeting he had told her to call him Jimmy, which, he said, all his friends did.

'And John Burstine I'm sure you know,' the Sultan said, indicating the red-faced Englishman.

Burstine nodded and twiddled his grey moustache. 'Yes, I know Susan quite well.'

Susan smiled at him. He was an airline manager and an Old Singapore Hand, or so he claimed.

The Sultan raised one hand. 'Let me get you a drink, Miss York.'

A waiter appeared at the Sultan's side almost instantly and Susan said she would have an orange juice. She knew the Sultan and Jimmy were Muslims and didn't—or weren't supposed to— drink alcohol. But she also knew they had no objection to non-Muslims like John Burstine drinking.

They chatted while the waiter brought Susan's drink. Jimmy sipped his orange juice glumly. He looked like he wasn't terribly interested in his elders' conversation, apart from not enjoying his orange juice. Susan knew from experience that Jimmy liked to drink when his father wasn't around. Like many young Muslims, Jimmy didn't adhere very strictly to some of the old beliefs. On marriage, he was very positive he would have only one wife, and not the four his religion permitted.

As they talked, Susan suddenly saw the Sultan's eyes light up and she turned and saw K.K. coming towards them, with Tanya gliding by his side and Greg McKenzie close behind.

Greg wore a creamy twill evening jacket with a cream silk shirt, black tie and black trousers. He looked very handsome in his tropical evening dress.

But the eyes of the men fixed themselves on Tanya. She wore a brief, chocolate-coloured camisole top encrusted with copper bugle beads. A loop of fine gold chains hung to her bare, tanned midriff, ending above a flowing skirt in light brown chiffon, cut almost to the thigh on one side. Her dark hair was coiled sleekly, with one lock falling over her bare shoulder. She smiled radiantly, conscious she was the focus of male eyes.

Susan groaned inwardly, but forced a smile as Tanya and K.K. approached with Greg.

K.K. performed the introductions and the group formed a wider circle as waiters glided around bringing drinks for K.K., Tanya and Greg. The waiters also took orders for fresh drinks for the Sultan, Jimmy, Burstine and Susan.

In the confusion of greetings and introductions, Jimmy whispered to Susan, 'Order a gin and orange this time.'

She frowned at him, but she did so, while Jimmy, like his father, ordered another orange juice.

When the drinks arrived, Jimmy waited until his father was absorbed in talking to Tanya and K.K., then he quickly took Susan's glass of gin and orange and surreptitiously handed her his. He grinned and whispered, 'This is more your kind of drink—and this is more mine.'

He smiled at her and took a long drink of his gin-laced orange.

Greg, who had been talking with John Burstine, moved closer to Susan and Jimmy after another guest came up and buttonholed Burstine.

Greg smiled. 'I saw that switch,' he said quietly to Susan. 'You leading Jimmy astray?'

Jimmy took another sip of his gin and orange. 'No,' he said, 'it's I who would like to lead Susan astray. At Cambridge, I was known as the hell-raiser of King's.'

Greg laughed. 'I guess you're making hay while the sun shines.'

'Yes,' Jimmy said soberly. 'When I succeed the old man I don't expect it'll be a life of wine, women and song—not for Sultans these days.'

Greg asked Jimmy a question about the State he would one day rule, and Susan listened until David strolled over from the patio and joined them.

'I think everybody who's been invited has arrived,' he said, 'so I can stop being acting host. I'll have a drink, then join K.K. and the Sultan.'

A waiter glided up and took David's order. Jimmy murmured to Susan to repeat her previous order, which when it arrived, he again switched with her so he ended with the gin and orange.

Greg said to Susan, as David and Jimmy moved towards the Sultan's group, 'You sure won't get high tonight, will you? Looks like you're stuck with orange juice.'

She said, 'That's what I prefer. I don't drink much.'

He grunted. 'Not like young Jimmy.'

She laughed. 'He's really just an overgrown schoolboy. In spite of his sophistication, he can be very immature sometimes. But I must keep an eye on him—his father would be furious if he knew he was drinking alcohol.'

Greg nodded. 'You seem to like him. And he likes you.'

She smiled. 'I've taken groups to his palace about six times. He's quite different at home and he takes his duties as a host very seriously. But when he gets away from the palace he tends to kick up his heels. He's only twenty-two,' she added. 'Two years younger than me.'

David left the Sultan's group and joined Susan and Greg.

David said, 'Tanya's doing some good work with His Highness.' He nodded towards Tanya in the centre of an animated group which included K.K., Burstine and another two guests as well as the Sultan and Jimmy.

Susan sniffed. 'Surrounded by six men—that'll make Tanya happy!'

David smiled. 'That's about par for the course for Tanya. The more males around, the more she scintillates.'

Susan glanced up at Greg, whose eyes had wandered over her head to where Tanya was holding court. Susan took a sip of her drink, then said, striving for lightness, 'You'll have her all to yourself on the tour. And you'll be in Malacca tomorrow night. It's very romantic there.'

After she had said it, she wished she hadn't. David frowned at her, but Greg only shrugged. He said, 'As a matter of fact, I was watching young Jimmy. He's organised his own supply of spiked drinks from one of the waiters and he's getting a touch high. If he doesn't watch it, his old man's going to tumble to what he's drinking.'

David and Susan looked at Jimmy, who was standing with Burstine near the Sultan, who was talking with Tanya. Jimmy was teetering back and forward on his heels, trying to look grave while concentrating on a monologue Burstine was delivering. Like Burstine, Jimmy was obviously well oiled.

Susan said, 'He probably sneaked a few before he came here. He doesn't really like this kind of party. There aren't many people of his age.'

Greg nodded. 'No, it's not the kind of party a young guy would enjoy. It's not exactly swinging.'

Susan said, 'I think I should join him. I might be able to get him back on to straight orange juice before his father tumbles to him.'

She smiled at David and Greg, then strolled across to the Sultan's group where she edged herself close to Jimmy, who promptly put an arm round her then cuddled her affectionately.

Gently Susan forced him from her and held one

of his hands. She said to Burstine, 'You don't mind if I take Jimmy away to talk about England?'

'But that's what we *were* talking about!' Burstine exclaimed. 'I was telling Jimmy about my days at Oxford.'

Susan knew Burstine had never been at Oxford. Although he had worked at an Oxford travel agency, where he had picked up enough knowledge of the city to pass himself off as an Oxford graduate. Which he did when he was tipsy.

She smiled at him winningly. 'We're going to talk about Cambridge. I've been there a few times.'

Burstine twirled his moustache. 'Cambridge, eh? Well, that cuts me out. I'll have another Scotch.' He waved an unsteady hand towards a waiter.

Susan smiled across the lawn at Tanya, who smiled back serenely. She was being very ladylike in the presence of His Highness. Susan drew Jimmy by the hand away from the group and led him around the pool to a cushioned recliner where she sat down, then drew him down beside her.

He held his glass carefully between his knees and looked at her owlishly. She said quietly but severely, 'You're getting drunk. In fact, you are drunk.'

His eyes sharpened slightly. 'Oh, is it noticeable?'

She smiled. 'Well, I noticed—and so did others. Your father will probably be next to notice. So you'd better begin sobering up.'

'All right,' he said obediently, draining his glass, then shaking his head vigorously. 'It's time

I got off this stuff anyway, and switched to champagne.'

Susan said, 'That would be a bit obvious, wouldn't it?'

He shook his head. 'You don't appreciate the subtleties of the Muslim religion. Or my father's interpretation of it anyway. You see, my father rather likes champers. He classes it as wine, not alcohol, and a few glasses of champagne are permissible—for himself, and even for me. So let's find some.'

He jumped to his feet, then stood steady himself for a moment. He held out one hand and Susan rose reluctantly to her feet and smoothed her skirt. She finished her orange juice, then put her glass down beside Jimmy's on a small white table. A waiter came past carrying a tray on which was a bottle of champagne in an ice bucket and several glasses.

Jimmy signalled him and said, 'Thank you,' and took the bottle and two glasses from the tray.

The waiter bowed and Jimmy motioned Susan to follow him away from the pool towards a more secluded seat. She strolled after him, conscious of K.K.'s eyes following them. They sat down together and Jimmy poured two glasses of champagne and handed her one.

He clinked glasses with her, then drank most of his champagne in one gulp. Susan sipped some of hers, then said, 'This is not my idea of how you should sober up.'

Unsteadily, Jimmy refilled his glass, while Susan watched him, occasionally glancing anxiously across the pool to where the Sultan stood with Tanya, K.K. and David.

Several times, waiters crossed the lawn and approached Susan and Jimmy with trays of canapés. Susan had a few bites, but Jimmy waved the food away.

'It's Ramadan,' Jimmy told one of the Chinese waiters, 'the fasting month for Muslims. I cannot eat.'

Susan prodded him. 'You know it's not Ramadan—that's later in the year, And anyway, even at Ramadan you only fast from sunrise to sunset.'

He looked owlishly at her, his smooth olive brow showing a few beads of perspiration. 'You're becoming very smart, Miss York, about our native Malay customs.'

'I have to be,' she said, 'you forget that I'm expected to know about these things when I'm escorting the tours.'

He signalled a hovering waiter and asked for another bottle of champagne.

Susan frowned, for she hadn't even finished her first glass, which meant Jimmy had drunk most of the bottle. She said firmly, 'I think you've had enough. It might be a good idea if we slipped quietly into the house and you went to the bathroom and dunked your head in some cold water.' She jumped to her feet. 'Come on—we'll stay close together and I'll guide you—discreetly.'

She pulled him to his feet, protesting, and drew him across the lawn. As they walked slowly towards the pool, the waiter who had taken Jimmy's order came towards them carrying a fresh bottle of champagne, already opened, on a tray.

The waiter stopped close to them and Susan indicated that they didn't want the champagne. But Jimmy stepped forward and grabbed the bottle from its bucket on the tray.

'Thank you,' he said, and raised the bottle to his mouth and began drinking.

Embarrassed, and fearful of the Sultan seeing him, Susan tried to pull the bottle away, but Jimmy clung to it, until he had swigged down several mouthfuls. Then he threw an arm round her waist and began dragging her towards the path that surrounded the pool then curved up to the house.

'Come on!' he cried, tucking the bottle under his arm, when some of the contents foamed out over his pants. Susan gritted her teeth, then locked her arm round him to steady him and together they weaved their way towards the pool.

Unlike Jimmy, Susan was completely sober. By herself, she could have walked perfectly sedately towards the house, but arm in arm with the tottering Jimmy, they looked from a distance like a couple of drunks staggering along supporting one another.

She tried to free herself from his clinging arm and walk by herself, but he kept his arm coiled around her waist as he pulled her towards the pathway fringing the pool.

On the other side of the sparkling water, Susan saw the Sultan, K.K., David, Tanya and Greg all looking at her and Jimmy. She smiled weakly across at them, trying to indicate that she was merely helping Jimmy.

She saw the grim expression on the Sultan's smooth features as he realised his son was more than mildly inebriated. Susan knew that to the Malays, as well as to the Chinese, what was known as 'face' was still extremely important. And Jimmy's behaviour was not only causing him to lose face, but it reflected on his father.

Desperately she tried to free herself from Jimmy as they drew closer to the pool. She didn't want to get too near the edge, because she thought he might fall in—or even throw himself in for a lark.

As they reached the pool parapet, she twisted in his arms and jerked herself away vigorously. But Jimmy clutched the side of her sleeveless jacket under her arm, there was a loud ripping sound and the flimsy material of the jacket was torn apart.

Frantically Susan clutched the torn lace round herself and gave Jimmy a slight push to make him release his grip on the strip of material he was still grasping. He let the cobwebby lace go, but her push caused him to stagger back and there were cries from several guests as Jimmy, still clutching the champagne bottle, spreadeagled backwards into the pool and hit the water with a loud splash.

Susan stood quivering with embarrassment and horror, and gathered the tattered jacket around herself as Jimmy thrashed about in the water, yelling with delight. Waiters hurried up and knelt by the pool, reaching out to him with their hands. But Jimmy floated serenely on his back, shaking water from his eyes and calling to Susan to join him.

Susan clutched the torn lace to her bosom,

noting that several of the guests were inching nearer to have a look at the scene she had become involved in. From the other side of the pool. K.K. was striding furiously towards her. He was followed by the Sultan, his brow black, and Tanya, David and Greg.

K.K. reached her first and hissed, 'I am furious with you, Susan! What an incredible spectacle you've made of yourself! And with His Highness's son! I am absolutely disgusted and ashamed——'

He stopped abruptly as the Sultan came up and halted suddenly. The stocky Malay ruler glanced coldly at Susan, then averted his eyes quickly as she tugged her torn jacket closer round herself. Then, majestically, the Sultan turned and surveyed his splashing son.

He didn't say a word to Jimmy, who stopped floundering as he met his father's furious gaze. The Sultan raised his arm imperiously and pointed towards the house. Then he turned to K.K. and said, 'My apologies, Mr Koh. To yourself and your guests. I am deeply humiliated.'

Then he turned on his heel and strode past them. His face pale, K.K. hurried after him.

Slowly, Jimmy turned on to his front and began swimming breast-stroke towards the other side of the pool.

David strode up, slipped off his white dinner jacket and draped it round Susan's bare shoulders. His brow was dark as she pulled the jacket closer round her front.

Tanya sauntered up and said sweetly, 'This reminds me of a Gidget movie. Or Suzy Gets High

With the Sultan's Son.'

Behind Tanya Susan saw Greg. His face was grave, but she thought she saw the faintest trace of amusement lurking in his eyes as he looked at her.

'I am not drunk!' Susan snapped. 'Jimmy was drunk and I was trying to sober him up.'

Greg said, 'Champagne can be insidious—if you're not used to it.'

'I only had one glass!' she flared at him. 'Not even that.'

K.K. came hurrying back from escorting the Sultan out and he pushed through the group and halted, facing Susan.

He said to Greg, 'I apologise for all this. My parties don't usually degenerate into this kind of——' he glanced at Susan with distaste—'drunken behaviour.'

Greg pursed his lips. 'I don't think Susan was drunk, K.K. I thought——'

'I don't need anyone to defend me!' Susan snapped. She drew David's jacket tighter round herself. 'Goodnight, Mr Koh,' she said, tossing her head.

She turned, and with as much dignity as she could muster she strode through the guests, looking straight ahead.

At the gate, she strode past the Sikh watchman towards David's car, until she remembered she didn't have its keys. But she wasn't going to wait for him to drive her. All she wanted was to get home and start thinking about getting another job. Or else making her departure from Singapore in a hurry.

CHAPTER FIVE

SUSAN sat in the jump seat of Tiger Tours' newest air-conditioned Mercedes Benz coach as it cruised through dense groves of rubber trees on the road from Singapore to Malacca. Beside her, gripping the wheel, was Munir, his brown face intent as he piloted the silver and yellow coach along the sun-dappled highway that ran north to the Thai border, over four hundred miles away.

Her seat faced the rear of the coach so she could look along the aisle and see the passengers and be seen by them as she talked quietly through her microphone.

There were only eighteen passengers, although the coach could take twenty-eight in relaxed comfort. But it was slightly better than a break-even load, so Tiger Tours wouldn't lose on this five-day trip up the Malay peninsula.

Only seven hours had elapsed since Susan had first met her passengers when they gathered in Singapore to board the coach, but she had already mentally classified them as 'a good crowd'. Her tour group included five Americans, four English people, two New Zealanders, two Canadians, two Swiss, two Germans and one Japanese.

Susan sat with her knees and ankles neatly together, displaying her shapely legs in white, medium-heeled shoes. She wore her tour conductor's uniform of knee-length grey skirt, white open-necked blouse and short yellow jacket.

Because of the amount of bending, kneeling and stretching she had to do on the coach, Susan would have preferred to wear slacks. But K.K. insisted that the girls wore skirts. He said Malay males didn't like seeing women in trousers. As a Muslim society, it was very male-dominated, and the Malay women still mainly wore the traditional *sarong*, or modernised versions of it like the *sarong kebaya*.

The *sarong* was also more concealing than a short skirt, she reflected, conscious of masculine eyes on her from a few feet away. She glanced up at one of the five American passengers, and it was Greg's gaze she met as he sprawled in the first two seats near the door and to her right. Through half-closed eyes he surveyed her, then he smiled.

She smiled back, then bent her head and pretended to study the passenger list. She wondered how she was going to concentrate on her job for the next five days, with Greg facing her most of the time in his seat a few feet away.

It was thanks to him she was on this tour—and probably thanks to him she still had a job.

After the disastrous scene at K.K.'s party, she had gone home by taxi, David's jacket around her. In her apartment she had got out of her ruined lace top. She had been burning with rage, embarrassment, and above all, resentment at what had happened. The torn, expensive top was the final straw.

She had lain dejectedly on her bed, sombrely contemplating her future—or lack of it—when just after midnight the phone rang. It was David.

He had told her briefly that she should get packed and report in the morning to take tomorrow's tour north.

She couldn't believe it at first, telling him she had been expecting to get the sack. He confirmed that she had come close to it, but Greg had specially requested that she conduct tomorrow's tour—the one he would be sampling.

David told her they had had a long discussion in K.K.'s study after the last guest had gone. Greg had invited himself into their discussion, and K.K. had let him because he didn't want to offend him and jeopardise any business Greg's company might eventually give Tiger Tours.

It was for the same reason that K.K. had agreed to let Susan go on her scheduled tour. In addition, before midnight K.K. had received an apologetic phone call from a very sober and chastened Jimmy, who had gone to some lengths to explain that Susan hadn't been drunk, but had indeed been trying to stop him drinking any more and tried to steer him up to the house to sober up.

When Susan met Greg in the morning as he arrived at Tiger Tours Singapore departure lounge with the other passengers, she had thanked him for requesting her as tour conductor.

'Forget it,' he said briefly. 'You got a bad break last night.'

'Yes,' she said feelingly, 'I seem to have had more than my share of bad breaks since I met you.'

Then her hand flew to her mouth as she realised how ungracious her words sounded.

He laughed. 'This is Day Three of our acquaintanceship. It's got to go better.'

And, Susan reflected, as she glanced at him sprawled across his two seats, it certainly had gone better—so far.

Greg had really tried to be a good tourist. He had listened intently as she had made her welcoming speech to the passengers as the coach cruised up the Bukit Timah Road to the Johore Causeway which linked Singapore and Malaya.

She had explained that as their tour conductor, she was responsible for every aspect of the arrangements as well as being their guide and commentator. She told them that if they had any problems—day or night—they were not to hesitate about calling her.

'At our hotels, I'll tell everybody my room number, but the desk will always be able to contact me if I'm not in my room. During the tour, I'm never off duty and I'll do my best to comply with any special requests.'

The Japanese passenger's eyes had gleamed at that, so she had frowned at him severely to indicate that there was a limit to the services she would perform. Chastened, he had lowered his eyes behind his thick spectacles.

One of the passengers, a large middle-aged American lady from Toledo, Ohio, travelling with her husband, a wiry little man in his late fifties, had called out to Susan, 'That's a bit tough on you, honey. You've got to get your beauty sleep.'

Her husband promptly added, 'She don't need it! She's beautiful enough, Maimie.'

Susan had warmed to the couple—Mr and Mrs

Eikhorn, or Luke and Maimie as they insisted she should call them.

Susan had explained various arrangements for the tour and also given them a brief run-down on their itinerary. Tonight they would stay at Malacca, then on successive nights at Kuala Lumpur, Ipoh, Khedar Palace, then on the fifth day they would reach Penang.

Since leaving Singapore and entering Malaya, they had made a morning refreshment stop, a couple of stops for photography and a longer stop for lunch at a little village off the main road near Bata Phat.

After a light lunch of mild Malay curry at an atmospheric *kedai kopi* or coffee shop utilised by Tiger Tours, she had shepherded her charges around the kampong to have their first experience of Malay village life. She had used her Malay quite frequently to interpret for the clients, because away from the big cities, fewer Malays spoke English.

In the market-place she had shown them the tropical Malayan fruits, many of them strange to Westerners. There were mangosteens, which the Malays called the Queen of Fruits; little rambutans with their soft, hairy prickles; belembing or star-fruit; delicious langsats; grapefruit-like pomelos, and of course, papaya and pineapple of which Malays is a big exporter.

Maimie Eikhorn tried a slice of pineapple and reported that it was quite different from the sweeter Hawaiian pineapple.

Greg had followed the rest of the passengers as Susan led them round the market, and she was very conscious of him always close, although never crowding her.

As she explained the fruits and told her charges that they were quite safe to eat, she picked up a large, prickly-looking fruit and told them it was the durian, which the Malays called the king of fruits.

Munir, who had been walking round with the group and occasionally translating something that was too difficult for Susan, smiled when she mentioned the durian.

Susan said, 'The durian has a very strong smell. But it tastes as nice as its smell is bad.' She hesitated, then went on, 'In Malaysia it's renowned for having very stimulating properties.'

Munir explained, 'There's an old Malay saying that when the durians ripen and fall, the maidens' sarongs will also fall.'

Everyone laughed and there was some mildly ribald remarks. Susan blushed slightly, for she knew the Malay saying was somewhat pithier than Munir's edited version. She glanced at Greg and he murmured to her, 'That's very interesting. Do you ever eat durians?'

'No,' she said, her cheeks becoming pinker, 'and I don't very often wear a sarong.'

Luke Eikhorn bought four of the durians. He winked as he clutched the exotic love fruit. 'I'm going to feed them to Maimie. She needs more pep!'

When they arrived in Malacca in the early afternoon, the picturesque old town was drowsing in the hot tropical sun. Munir drove the coach to

Bukit China and Susan led her group to a vewpoint on top of the hill.

She told them how Malacca had been a pirates' lair as far back as the Middle Ages, long before Columbus discovered America. Then it had been occupied by roving Chinese seafarers and become a trading centre and crossroads between Arabia and China. Then in 1511 the Portuguese took over Malacca and ruled until driven out by the Dutch in 1641. The Dutch were driven out in 1795 by the British, who ruled until Malacca became part of the independent Federation of Malaysia in 1963.

Munir took them for a short drive around the old town and Susan pointed out evidence of former rulers of Malacca. The old Dutch Town Hall, the Portuguese Porta de Santiago, the Chinese temple, Cheng Hoon Teng—or Bright Clouds Temple, and finally, the still very British Malacca Club, which Somerset Maugham wrote of at the height of the British colonial era.

Munir then drove the coach to the Gelombang Hotel, where Susan assembled her charges in the cool, high-ceilinged dining room for a traditional English afternoon tea under slowly-revolving overhead *punkah* fans. While they had tea, she supervised the transfer of the passengers' baggage from the coach to their rooms. Then she collected their keys, ready in envelopes with some literature about Malacca, and distributed them to her charges.

She explained that they were completely free for the evening, but in the morning they would do a comprehensive tour of the town and its surrounds before driving less than a hundred miles to

Malaysia's capital, Kuala Lumpur, which would be their next overnight stop.

She described a selection of places they might like to visit during the evening and stressed again that she was always on call if they wanted any special help or advice. Finally, as the passengers collected their keys and drifted away to their rooms, she sat down thankfully to have some tea herself.

Greg, who had been chatting with the Eikhorns, strolled over and sat beside her.

'So, apart from being on call for the tourists, I take it you're free for the evening?'

She nodded. 'I only have to rinse out some things and hang them up to dry. Laundry is quite a problem on these tours, as we never stop anywhere long enough to get any done by the hotels.'

'O.K.,' he said, 'then how about we go out for dinner someplace? I'll leave the choice to you—obviously you know the best places.'

She hesitated. 'I'd like to go out, but I don't really like leaving the hotel. As I said, I'm on duty all the time—at least until they've all gone to bed.'

He nodded. 'Right, then it looks like we have dinner here in the hotel.'

'I'd love that. But I don't want you to be tied down just because I have to be.'

Greg smiled. 'I think I could stand being tied down with you—for one night anyway!'

Susan turned pink and buried her face over her tea cup.

He asked, 'Do you have a key for me?'

'Yes.' She handed it to him. 'You're in the best suite. The manager, Mr Tan, will be looking after you personally when he gets back from a meeting he's at. You're going to get the VIP treatment.'

Greg nodded. 'I'm used to that, I guess. People in the travel business always try to make sure I enjoy all the—facilities.'

He looked at her deadpan and she rose quickly and gathered up her things.

'I—I must go,' she said.

He asked her room number, then said he would give her a call after she had settled in. As they walked to the elevator, the manager, Mr Tan, came bustling in from his meeting in town and apologised for not being in the hotel to greet Mr McKenzie. Susan talked with them for a few minutes, then excused herself and left Greg in the manager's hands.

She smiled commiseratingly at Greg as Mr Tan dragged him off for 'a quick tour of our lovely hotel'.

In her room, she quickly unpacked and hung her dresses, then got out of her uniform and washed some things. She had a shower, then while doing her hair she got the first of several calls from members of her tour group. Their enquiries ranged from finding adaptors for electrical appliances to where to buy a German-made stomach powder. Such calls were routine for Susan and they always came when she was trying to look after her own needs. But she answered them all cheerfully and politely and was generally able to help them with their problems.

At six-thirty she was trying to get dressed after being held up by more calls. But by seven o'clock she managed to get everything together.

She wore a luminous blue ottoman jacket and skirt. The jacket skimmed her hips and under it she wore no bra. The silk felt cool against her bosom. The narrow skirt was in a modified tulip shape and her slender waist was emphasised by a yellow sash. She wore dazzling open-toed shoes in metallic blue. She had done her hair in a soft, wavy sweep that fell almost to her shoulders.

Studying herself in the mirror, she thought she looked rather different from the trim, efficient Susan whom Greg had seen all day in the coach. She had packed the blue outfit earlier that morning after David had told her she was back on the tour. She remembered that she had worn her blue shirt-dress in Singapore when she had had lunch with Greg at the Mandarin, and he had told her the colour suited her. She was glad he liked her in blue, for it was one of her favourite colours.

At five past seven her phone rang, and it was Greg. 'I've just escaped from Mr Tan,' he told her. 'He's shown me everything, from the wine cellars to the air-conditioning plant on the roof—and the kitchens. And he desperately wanted to have dinner with me—and you too, of course. But I don't fancy a night of heavy hotel sales promotion over dinner, so I told him I had to stay in my suite and write up some reports.'

'Oh?' she said.

'It was only an excuse,' he said lightly. 'But now I can hardly eat in the dining room with you or he'd know about it for sure and be insulted. So how about we dine up here? It's a great suite, and it's got a balcony with a terrific view of Malacca.'

'All right,' she said. 'I'll tell them at the desk that I'll be in your suite if anyone wants me.'

Greg told her to come right on up and they'd have a drink before dinner; Susan said she would, then hung up.

Dinner alone with him in his suite! Well, she thought ruefully, that'll be the end of my reputation with the hotel staff! Like hotel employees all over the world, the discreet Chinese house boys knew exactly where guests spent their evenings—and who with, in which rooms, and how long they stayed. Then Mr Tan—he'd hear about it for sure.

She shrugged as she finished doing her face. Ah well, it would be the first time in her years of touring that she had gone alone to a male passenger's room. Or had a man in her room either. Mr Tan and his staff would probably be gratified to know that the cool, poised Miss York could weaken and become human!

She told herself she had better be very careful tonight, for she had been disturbingly conscious of Greg close to her all day. She was sure he was interested in her; he would hardly have asked K.K. to let her conduct the tour if he wasn't. Not that he had said or done anything that could be construed as personal. But he had rarely taken his eyes off her and she had had the greatest difficulty in concentrating on her commentary.

As he had lolled back in his seat he had reminded her of a powerful tiger, which for reasons of its own was relaxing while it contemplated its next victim. At times, his dark grey eyes had an almost hypnotic affect on her and she felt like a helpless lamb waiting for the tiger to pounce.

She gave a little shiver of mingled apprehension and excitement as she combed her hair. Here she was, preparing to walk into the tiger's lair! She thought shakily that she better make sure he was well fed, for she remembered how on that first day in Singapore he had become considerably more human after he had lunch. Although when he became human he was really most dangerous, because then she dropped her defences, as she had done during their second lunch at the Mandarin. Greg had been very charming then, as he had been all today.

She thought he was really much easier to handle when he was being overbearing and arrogant. At least she then didn't have such disturbing thoughts and wonder what it would be like to be held in his arms and have his lips fused against hers. Somehow she wouldn't visualise him as a gentle lover, or even as an especially patient one. He looked as if he was used to getting exactly what he wanted—in his business and personal life. And getting it quickly. All that VIP treatment he took for granted.

Well, she reflected as she smoothed her jacket, he was due for a shock if he thought she was going to fall into his arms just because he was important to her company. When she gave herself to a man it would be because she wanted to—and because she was in love.

She stared at her reflection in the mirror and wonder if it could even be vaguely possible that she was falling for him. Then she shook herself vigorously. No, it was just physical attraction—

very powerful physical attraction, such as she had never felt before for any man. She really hadn't stopped thinking about him since they had first met on that disastrous Singapore tour.

Well, she concluded, she would be on her guard and quickly put him in his place if he thought he had had her assigned to this tour for his pleasure at each nightly stopover!

When she reached Greg's suite he opened the door, and she gulped when she saw he was dressed only in a bathtowel tucked round his waist.

'Come in,' he said. 'I've just had a shower, but I'll be with you in a minute.'

She glanced at his bare brown torso and re-membered every rippling muscle from the day they had met when he had stripped off his jacket to change the wheel. But this time she could also see his powerful legs under the towel as he padded across the carpet to the small bar near the sliding windows in the big sitting room.

There was an assortment of bottles behind the bar with an ice bucket on top of a small re-frigerator.

Greg waved one arm. 'All with Mr Tan's com-pliments. Plus——' he waved towards a cane table beside a batik-covered divan—'more fruit than ten guys could eat!'

Susan glanced at the big lacquer bowl of tropical fruit on the table. She smiled, 'He's even given you durians.'

He laughed. 'Yeah. I wonder how Luke is doing feeding them to Maimie?'

'I wish I hadn't told everyone that old folk tale,'

she said lightly. 'They might expect too much from a simple fruit.'

He grinned. 'Let me make you a simple drink, then I'll get dressed. What would you like?'

'I'll just have vermouth and ice,' she said. 'I feel like something to pick me up. I didn't get much sleep last night, what with one thing and another.'

He busied himself making her drink. 'You look very lovely,' he said, eyeing her slim figure in the clinging blue silk that flowed enticingly over her curves. 'My favourite colour again. It makes you look really cool.'

He gave her the vermouth, then excused himself and padded into the bathroom.

Susan sipped her drink, then wandered across the sitting room and peeped into the separate bed-room. Greg had laid some clothes over the big double bed and his opened suitcase was lying on a stand. She strolled across to the bed and leaned over and pressed it with the palm of one hand, testing the mattress for firmness.

She jumped when a hand smacked her playfully on the rump and she whirled round. Greg, still draped in the towel, had padded up behind her. He grinned. 'Soft enough?' he enquired, nodding towards the bed.

She flushed. 'No—it's quite hard if anything. I hope you sleep well on it.'

He smiled. 'I expect I will.' He began to undo the towel tucked at his waist. 'Do you plan to stick around while I get dressed?' he enquired.

Susan scampered hurriedly past him. 'No,' she said, 'I'll wait outside.'

She scurried into the sitting room, then out on to the balcony and let the cool evening air blow over her hot face. She wondered again if this was really such a good idea, coming to his suite for dinner. She hoped he hadn't taken it the wrong way. But he knew she couldn't leave the hotel—and he wouldn't go with her to the dining room, or any of the hotel's public rooms, or Mr Tan would grab him and monopolise him. She wondered if Mr Tan would really be so persistent, or if Greg McKenzie had very glibly dreamed it up as an excuse to have an intimate dinner alone with her in his suite.

She finished her vermouth quickly and stopped thinking about Greg's possible duplicity. But she found it hard to stop thinking about his lean masculinity in his casually-draped towel.

She went into the sitting room and walked towards the bar as Greg came out of the bedroom. He wore slacks and an open-necked cotton shirt and a pair of loafers.

He smiled at her. 'Big casual night—not like last night in a monkey jacket.' He walked behind the bar and mixed himself a Martini, then poured a vermouth and held it out to her. 'You will have another?' he queried.

She nodded and took the glass, then perched herself on a bar stool facing him.

Greg drank some of his Martini, then said, 'O.K., about dinner. I'm famished—how about you?'

'Moderately hungry. I never eat much during the day, so I look forward to dinner at night.'

He picked up the Room Service menu from the bar top and said, 'Let's see what they can offer.'

They leisurely discussed the menu, which was quite comprehensive. Finally they settled on a crab appetiser, then a local fish called *terubok*, which Susan recommended. She also suggested Greg might like *assam sintang*, a shellfish served pickled, and Greg said he would go along with whatever she thought. 'We might as well stay with fish, being right on the sea.'

He gave the order over the phone and also asked for a bottle of champagne. 'I guess champagne will go with your exotic seafood,' he said to her as he replaced the receiver.

Susan put down her glass. 'In that case I won't have any more vermouth.' Then she smiled. 'I'm surprised you have the nerve to offer me champagne, after what it did to Jimmy last night!'

Greg cocked his head. 'I guess one glass won't do you any harm.'

She nodded. 'No, I rather like champagne. It's one of the few alcoholic drinks I do like.'

They talked together while waiting for their meal to come up. Mainly they talked about the other passengers and their reaction to the tour so far.

Susan said, 'We do some fairly hard sightseeing tomorrow, and we have an early start. So I hope all my people get to bed early tonight.'

There was a discreet tap on the door, then three smiling Chinese waiters entered with dinner and set it up on a table on the balcony overlooking the lights of the town. It was cooler than it had been in Singapore and the night breeze from the Straits of Malacca was soft and balmy.

The head waiter asked if they wanted him to stay and serve dinner, but Greg said they would look after themselves. The waiter opened the champagne with a pop and set it in its ice bucket, then, bowing, he retreated from the suite.

They ate sitting across from one another, their knees almost touching, and Susan reflected that she had never known how romantic a Malacca night could be. Nor had she realised how delicious Malacca specialities could be.

Greg ate everything with relish and plied her with champagne, but she only drank two glasses. She stopped him when the bottle was empty and he suggested ordering another.

'No,' she said, 'I have to be up early tomorrow. And so do you,' she added. 'We leave for Kuala Lumpur at seven-thirty. Bags outside by seven.'

He smiled and put one hand over hers. 'No instructions tonight! Forget the tour conducting. Relax—let yourself go and enjoy the evening.'

They talked on over coffee. Greg asked her about her life in England and she told him more about herself. Then she got him talking too, and time flew until she realised with a start that it was after eleven o'clock.

She got up from the table reluctantly and said, 'I think it's time I went.'

He stood up and took her by the hand and queried, 'One nightcap before you go?'

Without waiting for an answer, he led her into the sitting room and over to the batik-covered divan, then gently pressed her shoulders until she let herself sink down and relax against the soft cushions. Then he took his hands away and straightened up. 'What'll it be?' he asked.

She smiled. 'Mineral water—I must be up early tomorrow.'

Greg nodded, then went to the bar and poured her mineral water and a glass of port for himself. He brought the drinks over and set them down on the small telephone table by the divan. Then he sat down beside her, stretching himself luxuriously. 'If the mineral water overwhelms you I promise I won't take advantage of you,' he said.

Susan glanced sideways at him. 'Then what is your arm doing round my shoulders?'

'Because it makes it easier for me to pull you closer—like this.' He drew her head down on to his shoulder, and his other arm went round her, drawing her tightly to him. 'Which, in turn, makes it easier for me to do something I've wanted to do all day—very badly.'

He bent his head and tilted her face, then kissed her tenderly on the lips. Susan melted against his chest and her arms went round him.

They kissed for a long time, and when Greg occasionally took his lips from hers it was to murmur endearments as he stroked her face and hair.

'I really should go,' she whispered, conscious of a warm stirring inside herself. 'This could very easily get out of hand.'

His eyes sought hers. 'How easily?' he murmured.

She tried to struggle free of his warm, enveloping

arms. 'Too easily,' she muttered, 'I——'

He stopped her mouth with kisses, then his hand played gently with her neck and he stroked her skin with feathery touches. His hand strayed down her neck to her slowly heaving bosom and her skin burned at his touch as she writhed, her thighs pressed tightly together.

Through the thin material of her jacket she felt his hand caress her breast and under the clinging silk her nipples tautened at his touch, betraying her rising passion.

Greg sighed and kissed her deeply as his hand slid inside her jacket to seek her swelling breasts. Tantalizingly he stroked them, his fingers delicately teasing her and causing her to writhe uncontrollably against his aroused body.

He took one of her hands and kissed her palm, then with his other hand he stroked her back. Then he crushed her to him and kissed her passionately. Susan gasped and struggled free of his lips and his hard, demanding body pressing against her yielding softness.

She forced him away and he let her, but he kept one arm around her neck, playing with her ear lobes, teasing her blonde hair and stroking the back of her neck with feather light touches that made her skin tingle and caused her to quiver with violent spasms of pleasure.

'I—I must go,' she panted, her bosom heaving. 'I'll—I'll never get up in the morning.'

Greg tried to pull her back into his arms. He muttered, 'I'll see you get up in the morning. I'll put in an early call.'

'No!' she said sharply, thrusting him away. 'I'm not—staying with you! I'm going back to my room.'

'Why?' he said tenderly. 'Don't you feel like I feel?'

She held him at arm's length. 'And how do you feel?' she said unsteadily.

'About you?'

She nodded, straining to hold herself away from him as he pulled her towards his demanding body.

He relaxed the tug of his arms and she sagged slightly, then quickly smoothed her hair with one free hand.

'Well——' he said slowly, 'let's say I've found you very—disturbing. You could even say I haven't been able to get you out of my mind since I first saw you slide out of that bus. Let's say I'd very much like to make love to you, right now.'

His tone was a combination of urgent demand and gentle pleading.

'Oh?' she said, tugging down her skirt which had crept to her thighs. 'Thank you. I know you want to make love to me—you've made that very clear! But I—I don't want to make love to you.'

Greg slid one hand behind her neck and gripped her by the hair, forcing her to look into his eyes.

'I think you're telling a lie,' he whispered. 'I think you do want me to make love to you.'

'I don't tell lies!' she said shortly, trying deliberately to be severe with him.

'Well, let's say you're telling a fib—is that better?' His eyes were amused as he studied her flushed face.

'I—I——' she shook her head to release her hair from his grip. 'I think this is just fun to you! I don't think you're—serious about me. Why should you be? To you I'm just a passing affair, aren't I?'

He untwined his fingers from her hair and looked at her frostily, his eyes smouldering suddenly. 'I think you're more than a passing affair. If I thought that, I assure you I'd be further advanced with you than I am now.'

'Oh, so you're being gentlemanly?'

'Not gentlemanly—gentle. And it's because I care for you very much.'

'Oh?' She stared at him, confused.

He made to draw her into his arms once more, but she tried quickly to get to her feet. The conversation was becoming very beguiling and dangerous and she felt she could easily get out of her depth and melt into his arms if he said any more. As she tried to get up he held her gently but firmly, then whispered, 'I'm sorry, I didn't mean it to be like this. I'd planned to take it slowly and be very tender and romantic.'

Susan stopped trying to break away from him. 'Oh? So you did have plans for tonight?'

He grinned suddenly and stroked her cheek. 'Well, let's say I planned to find out more about you—what kind of girl you are, etcetera. . . .'

'Hmm, I'm not sure about that etcetera. But have you found out enough about me?' Her eyes surveyed him coolly as she lay in his arms, her body tense.

He nodded. 'Yes, I've found out several things about you. One is that under that cool, English exterior, you're a very warm, exciting woman.'

'Oh!'

'And secondly, that even when you're aroused, you don't surrender too easily—or too often.'

She pushed him away and put her hands on her hips. 'I have not surrendered at all!' she said forcefully.

He grinned. 'I gathered that. So it looks like I'll have to revise my plans, if I'm going to have any hope of achieving my intentions.'

'Humph!' she snorted. 'I can guess what your intentions are!'

Greg smiled. 'There's one easy way to find out. Just relax, stop trying to get away, lie back, let me kiss you again, and I'll tell you all kinds of dreamy, romantic things.'

'I'm sure you're very good at that,' she said coolly. 'You've obviously had plenty of practice.'

'But not with a girl like you. Not even remotely like you. So I've got to go back to square one and brush up some wooing techniques that have become very rusty.'

'I'm sure you're very adaptable,' she said coldly. 'You must have a technique for every occasion.'

He shook his head. 'Not for this occasion. Because I haven't felt like this before about anyone.'

'Oh!'

She didn't resist as he took her gently into his arms and kissed her, a tender lingering kiss that made her melt against him. The forceful urgency he had displayed earlier had gone, and she found his gentleness more seductive than his ardent embraces of a few moments ago.

She tingled with growing desire as she returned his kisses and she was aware of his hands inside the cool silk of her jacket, stroking her burning skin. She moaned softly as she felt her defences slipping as her mind whirled into a vortex of passion. She gasped, then jumped as the telephone on the table beside the divan suddenly shrilled urgently.

'Oh!' she exclaimed.

Greg took a deep breath and frowned at the phone. 'We'll let it ring,' he said briefly.

Susan struggled up from the cushions. 'No—no, we can't. It might be for me. I have to answer it. Or I mean—you should answer it.'

He glanced at his watch. 'It's nearly midnight,' he said savagely. 'Who could want anything at this hour?'

She adjusted her jacket and said, 'Just answer it and find out. It may only be a query I can handle in a minute.'

Reluctantly, he reached for the phone and picked up the receiver. He said his name and listened for a moment, then thrust the receiver at her, an expression of disgust on his face.

'It's for you—Luke Eikhorn. Maimie's sick. She's got bad stomach pains.' He raised his eyes to the ceiling. 'You'd think they could call a doctor without bothering you.'

Susan took the receiver from him and said quickly, 'No, it's my responsibility. If she's too ill to travel tomorrow then I'll have to make all kinds of arrangements.'

She stared beseechingly at him, but he only looked at her darkly, his face set. Her hand trembled as she spoke into the phone to a very agitated Luke.

She talked for a moment, then said she would contact a doctor right away, then come down to their room and do what she could for Maimie. She put the phone down, picked it up again and told the desk to call a doctor and ask him to go to the Eikhorns' room. Then she jumped to her feet.

Greg had gone to the bar and poured himself a drink. He looked at her bleakly as she went towards him.

'I—I can't help it,' she said. 'I have to go to her. I—I'm very sorry, but I'm responsible for them.'

He nodded, his face dark. 'Fine,' he said curtly, 'then I suggest you don't waste any more time with me.'

Her heart sank. 'I—I'll see you tomorrow?' she whispered.

He grunted. 'We can hardly avoid it—if I decide to stay on the tour. At the moment, I'm more inclined to rent a car and go back to Singapore.'

Her face fell. 'Oh!' she protested. 'I thought you were—enjoying the tour.'

'I was. But I'd hoped to spend some time with you—and I don't mean sitting in a coach watching you being nice to seventeen other people.'

'But—but I have responsibilities. You must know that. You're being very unfair—and unreasonable! I must look after my passengers.'

Greg nodded. 'And I'm keeping you from your duty. So—goodnight.' He took a mouthful of his drink, turned his head and stared grimly out of the window.

Susan stamped her foot. 'You're a brute!' she cried. 'You've got no understanding at all! I'm certainly glad I found out what you're really like!'

He looked at the fury in her eyes, then said shortly, 'You'd better go. I'll tell you in the morning if I'm travelling on to Kuala Lumpur with you.'

She turned on her heel and strode furiously towards the door.

'Don't bother!' she snapped. 'It would be much better if you went back to Singapore. I certainly don't want to see you again!'

She wrenched the door open and ran out into the corridor.

CHAPTER SIX

SUSAN stood in front of the mirror in her room at the Merlin Hotel, Kuala Lumpur, and thought she rather liked the new, exotic Susan reflected in the amber-tinted glass.

She was dressed in the traditional full-length sarong worn by Malay women. She had bought it late in the afternoon at the market, after some good-natured haggling. Then, while she waited, she had had a few minor alterations done by a nimble-fingered Chinese seamstress.

She smoothed the sarong where it flowed over her hips and marvelled how the delicately pattern-ed batik garment gave her an almost Madonna-like grace—but with a serene sensuality that men found highly stimulating. Susan had read that de-scription of the sarong somewhere, and it had stayed in her mind. But until now she had never thought it particularly apt.

In her Singapore apartment she had two sarongs which she had bought soon after arriving in Malaysia. She had worn them a couple of times, but she had never thought they did anything for her. Her blonde English beauty was too much of a contrast with the exotic Eastern garment, and she had felt uncomfortably like a tourist apeing the graceful Malay women.

But tonight she thought the new sarong suited

her and that she had managed to blend East and
West rather well. Blonde Malay women were practically unknown, so Susan had covered her fair hair
with a midnight blue gossamer veil that floated
around her face and added a touch of mystery
which helped to transform an attractive Western
girl into a provocative Eastern beauty. The veil had
been the sarong saleslady's suggestion, and Susan
considered it two dollars well spent.

She had applied make-up carefully, using a light
tan foundation to give her creamy skin a golden
glow that suggested the Eastern sun, and highlight-
ed this with a melon-tinted blusher. She spent a
lot of time on her eyes, smudging them with dark
brown kohl-kajal pencil and a pale cream shadow
to present an allure appropriate to a sensual tropical night.

When she studied the overall affect in the mirror
it was like seeing the reflection of someone else.
She thought she looked pretty good, although she
was being characteristically modest. Actually, she
looked stunning.

She hoped when she arrived at his suite shortly,
Greg would think she at least looked—interesting.
She had bought the sarong especially for him, as
she wanted to please him after his handsome
apology for his behaviour the previous night.

He had knocked on the door of her room at
seven in the morning when she had just finished
packing her case ready to put it outside to be collected by the porters and taken to the coach. She
had been very pale and wan, as she had spent a
sleepless night, mainly thinking about him.

When she had opened the door he had strode in and taken her in his arms, and she hadn't resisted as he had kissed her very tenderly and gently stroked her hair.

Then he murmured, 'You were right last night. I was a brute—and a few other things as well. It was unforgivable of me to behave the way I did. My only defence is that I was bitterly disappointed at being interrupted, when I was trying to express my feelings. I was very upset—and like a fool, I took it out on you when you were only doing your job. Can you forgive me?'

Susan smiled tremulously. 'Yes, I do. I was also very—disappointed.'

Greg stroked her hair. 'But you handled it better than I did. I'm not very proud of myself.'

She stroked the back of his neck. 'Then you're coming on to Kuala Lumpur with us—with me?'

'Yes,' he smiled, 'I'll be staying with you until the end of the tour. So—dinner tonight in Kuala Lumpur?'

'Oh yes! And I hope my passengers don't bother me tonight.'

He grinned. 'I'll make sure they don't. Because this time I plan to unplug the telephone!'

He had kissed her again, then left her to organise the passengers on to the coach for the run to Kuala Lumpur.

Susan had immediately felt better and was very solicitous to Maimie Eikhorn. Ridiculously enough, last night's minor drama had been caused by Luke feeding durians to his wife, this giving her a violent tummy upset. Fortunately it had only been a brief attack, and after medication from the doctor, Maimie had rested until morning when she had insisted she would continue with the tour.

She had been very pale all day, and Susan had arranged extra cushions and placed her in two seats by herself so she could partially recline as the coach continued north to Kuala Lumpur.

When they had arrived at the Merlin Hotel, Maimie had gone straight to her room and lain down. Susan had visited her to check how she was, and she had said she expected to be fighting fit by next morning when they would travel north to Ipoh.

'But I won't be eating any more of the king of fruits,' she said coldly, glancing at her husband. 'Or anything else the king of fools tries to force on me.'

Luke patted her hand. 'It'll be hamburgers and French fries from here on,' he said.

But when they arrived at Kuala Lumpur, Maimie had insisted on staying with the group while they did a short tour of the city before driving to their hotel. 'I don't want to miss *anything*,' she explained.

She didn't get out of the coach with the others, but made Luke go so he could tell her all about it after each stop.

Susan had given them a fast tour of the capital, with its blend of ultra-modern and Eastern architecture. She had shown them the main railway station—which looked more like a Moorish temple. Then, in sharp contrast, they visited the new National Mosque—all stark, modern angles—

which, however, were very striking.

When the group strolled round the Mosque, Munir led the way, the men in the party walking with him. Susan and the women walked some way behind the males, in deference to Muslim custom. In addition, the women were issued with long black gowns that reached to their ankles. Everyone, men and women, removed their shoes as they walked round the holy place and saw the faithful at one of their four times daily prayers.

As they strolled among the pools and fountains in the Mosque's spacious grounds, dominated by its soaring minaret, Susan told the women about the Muslim religion, while ahead of them, Munir gave the same details to the men.

When they had completed the tour of the city and arrived at the hotel, Greg had been welcomed by the hotel manager and some of his executives, then dragged off for a tour of the hotel and its facilities. After her charges had been checked in, Susan gave them a briefing and told them they were going that night to a restaurant-entertainment complex at Petaling Jaya, where they would see a folk dance show, with a planned return to the hotel at eleven p.m. She gave them the assembly time in the lobby.

Later, Greg phoned from the suite he had been given and told her he had been forced to accept the manager's invitation to be his guest for dinner at the hotel. Susan explained that she had to dine at Petaling Jaya with the group, but she would be back in the hotel by eleven.

'O.K.,' he said, 'then I'll make sure I'm through

by eleven too. So how about us getting together someplace quiet? Like my suite? But this time, make certain your folks are all tucked in bed for the night!'

Susan had smiled into the receiver. 'I'll make very certain. I'll put knock-out drops in all their drinks!'

As she stood in her room surveying herself in her new sarong, she felt a delicious quiver of anticipation, for it was now half past eleven.

She had taken her group to their evening's dinner and entertainment, which they had enjoyed. Then Munir had driven them back to the hotel and she had said her goodnights and escaped to her room. She had pulled off the dress she had worn at the restaurant, then showered quickly, before donning the sarong. Greg had phoned while she was in the bathroom and she had told him she was getting dressed but would be ready in five minutes.

'That means half an hour!' he said. 'No woman has ever got dressed in five minutes.'

And he was right, she thought as she glided from her room in the sarong. Let's hope he thinks the wait was worth while.

As she rode in the elevator up to his suite, she reflected that this was the second time she had gone to his room. She knew she was deliberately playing with fire, and the thought made her tremble slightly with a mixture of apprehension and nerve-tingling excitement. But she doubted if anything could have kept her away from him tonight. She thought that last night he had been very close to telling her he loved her. He had confirmed it this morning when he had apologised and said he had been trying to express his feelings for her when they had been interrupted.

Her feelings towards him were now clear-cut. Last night, as she had tossed and turned in bed and wondered if he would continue on the tour, she realised she loved him. The thought of him disappearing out of her life had made her heart throb painfully and she had had to sit up in bed and take deep gasping lungfuls of air until her breathing returned to normal and her heart stopped pounding. She had never dreamed that being in love caused so many actual physical sensations—some delightful and others quite agonising.

But the worst sensation of all came when she contemplated never seeing him again. Then she was filled with an awful despair. She realised that in the few days she had known Greg she had experienced every kind of emotion, one after the other. But the most prevalent one was a desperate longing to be with him—and in his arms.

As she knocked lightly on the door of his suite she expected that within seconds she would be feeling his arms around her, and she trembled with anticipation.

But when she opened the door, he only took her hand and led her inside, then closed the door. He released her hand and stepped back and surveyed her in the graceful sarong and gossamer veil.

'You look very beautiful,' he said gravely. 'Like a completely different girl. I'll have to start getting to know you all over again.'

Susan laughed shakily, feeling the warmth of his

eyes on her. 'I haven't changed,' she said. 'It's still me.'

He nodded, then took her hand again and led her over to a large cane divan and she sat down. He didn't sit alongside her as she had expected. Instead, he sat in a matching cane armchair facing her.

'You really do look beautiful,' he said slowly. 'Very mysterious and exotic. I can hardly stop myself taking you into my arms and kissing you.'

She smoothed her sarong and said lightly, 'And why are you stopping yourself?'

He grinned. 'Two reasons. First, I thought we should get some things sorted out between us.'

'Oh? And the second reason?'

'A very simple one. If I took you in my arms right now then I'd probably pick you up, carry you through to the bedroom, and that would be the end of any intelligent conversation for the night.'

'Oh? And you want to make intelligent conversation?'

He nodded gravely. 'I do.'

Susan folded her arms in her lap and looked at him demurely. 'All right, I'm ready and waiting.'

He groaned, then jumped up and threw himself down on the divan beside her and took her in his arms. 'It's a waste of time,' he muttered. 'I had everything figured out, but I didn't count on seeing you dressed so—devastatingly! My mind's gone blank. All I know is that I want you!'

He covered her mouth with his lips and drew

her close and her heart hammered uncontrollably against his chest.

After a long minute she managed to draw her lips an inch away from his and murmur, 'What—what about this conversation?'

'Later,' he muttered, stroking the back of her neck with one hand while with one finger of the other he traced the line of her neck. 'I'll tell you lots of things later. Right now I'm going to make very tender love to you.'

His lips closed over hers and she melted into his arms and gave herself up to his kisses. After a little while she forgot all about conversation, intelligent or otherwise. New emotions of pure rapture surged over her as she responded to his passionate caresses. Almost in a trance, she clung to him as he fumbled delicately with the unfamiliar fastenings of her sarong, all the time kissing her mouth or murmuring into her ear while gently nibbling her lobes with his teeth. His tantalising caresses caused her to squirm wildly, and her entire body felt as if it was flowing with liquid heat.

Greg gently peeled the top of the sarong from her shoulders, then let it fall around her lap so that her bosom was exposed to his eyes—and to his tender touch. He bent his dark head and delicately kissed each breast in turn while she moaned in ecstasy.

He turned and faced her so his body pressed urgently against hers and she was blazingly con-scious of his desire. He pulled away and began ripping at his shirt buttons, murmuring, 'I want to get really close to you, my darling!' He tugged off his shirt, then his arms went round her and very gently he drew her soft bosom against his chest.

Susan struggled in his arms and made herself use every ounce of her willpower to force him away. She gazed into his eyes and murmured, 'You said once you began kissing me that would be the end of any conversation.'

He kissed her ear lobe and muttered, 'I said intelligent conversation.'

She wriggled her face away from his lips. 'I—I'd like to talk,' she said drowsily.

Greg gave a low groan. 'And I'd like to make love.'

'I know,' she said softly. 'It's love I'd like to talk about.'

He paused in his caresses and smiled. 'O.K., I do too. And tonight we don't have to worry about interruptions. No sick tourists this time?'

Susan smiled. 'No, there's no chance of that. I didn't tell anyone I was coming here. To be with you.'

He kissed her very tenderly, and simultaneously there was a loud knocking at the door.

He raised his head sharply and stared in utter disbelief at the door. Susan struggled into a sitting position and looked at him wide-eyed.

'Who on earth could it be?' she whispered.

The knock sounded again. It was a peremptory, commanding knock, not the discreet tap of a hotel servant.

Greg jumped to his feet, his eyes snapping, and said harshly, 'I'll damned soon find out—and I'll give whoever it is a blast! Some hotel!'

He strode towards the door as Susan called out,

'Shouldn't you put your shirt on?'

He paused. 'What for? This is *my* suite! You stay where you are, I'll get rid of them in a minute!'

But Susan quickly began pulling her sarong around herself and doing it up. As she struggled to her feet she heard Greg wrench open the door. Then her heart gave a sickening lurch as she heard David's voice, cool and slightly apologetic, but nevertheless, determined.

'Oh—hello, Greg,' she heard David say. 'Very sorry to bother you, but I believe Susan's with you. And she's wanted rather urgently.'

Susan moved slowly from the divan so she could see Greg at the open door with David outside, facing him. Then bitterness rose in her throat as behind David she saw Tanya, smiling coolly at Greg as he faced them both.

Susan said, 'Yes, I'm here.' She moved towards them. 'What do you want—and what are you doing here?'

She quickly smoothed her hair, conscious of her crumpled appearance and Greg's naked torso.

Greg stepped back abruptly and David took a hesitant pace into the room. David glanced at Susan as she stood with her head high, facing him.

An expression bordering on distaste showed on David's pale face as he looked at her.

'You didn't advise the desk where you would be,' he said shortly. 'But I found out from one of the hotel boys. Actually, it was only confirmation of where I expected you'd be.' His expression of distaste deepened. 'But,' he went on, 'I did think you'd do your job and leave word so clients would know where to find you in an emergency.'

Greg said shortly, 'And has there been an emergency?'

David looked at him expressionlessly. 'Rather,' he said. 'Two of Susan's passengers—a German couple—went out to a night club and apparently were ripped off. They wanted to see Susan to find out what could be done about it. They're down at the desk now and we're trying to sort things out.' He grimaced. 'It was lucky Tanya and I arrived when we did. At least *someone* from the company was on the job to handle things.'

Greg glanced at Susan, who said nothing, her mind a whirl of confusion and guilt. He asked, nodding to Tanya, who slipped into the room and smiled sweetly at Susan, 'And what brought you from Singapore so unexpectedly?'

'Various reasons,' David said shortly. 'I'll explain them to Susan—in due course.' He glanced at her. 'In the meantime, perhaps she could come down to the desk and look after her passengers. Tanya and I have had a long hard drive from Singapore today and would like to get some rest.'

Susan nodded dumbly and started towards the door.

David stood aside to let her pass, then said, 'It might be an idea if you went to your room first and changed. You do look rather like a—*houri* in that outfit.' His face was white and set as he looked at her.

Without a word she pushed past him and strode out of the room. As she went, she heard Tanya say lightly, 'Not a *houri*, David—they're professionals. I'd say Suzy looks more like a bazaar girl.'

CHAPTER SEVEN

SUSAN slumped listlessly in the jump seat and tried hard to keep her eyes open as Munir steered the coach around one of the many bends in the winding road that ran through the hilly jungle country between Bidor and Ipoh.

She was exhausted after the traumas of last night, and she had thought it would never end so she could snatch some sleep. But helping the German couple who had been ripped off at the club, plus later having to cope with David as he told her about *his* problems, had resulted in her getting precious little rest.

For various reasons, they had left Kuala Lumpur in the morning later than scheduled and stopped at Bidor for lunch. Now they were on the final stretch to Ipoh where they would spend the night. Susan hoped she wouldn't fall asleep and topple off the seat before they got there, she was so weary.

To complete her misery, instead of being able to look at Greg's rugged features as he lolled in the seats in front of her, it was a reproachful David who now occupied those seats. Greg—and she almost choked at the thought—was following the coach, alone in a Mercedes car driven by Tanya.

Munir swung the coach round a very tight bend and she had to grab the safety rail and hang on. Since they had left Kuala Lumpur the terrain had become rugged, even mountainous in parts, and on the right side of the coach ran the dense, jungle-clad ranges that formed a spine down inland Malaya.

Munir straightened the coach, then pulled off the road and brought the vehicle to a halt. Susan was forced to stop brooding about Greg and Tanya, alone in the following car, for it was time to show her passengers a tin-dredging operation.

As she walked around the tin-mining complex with her passengers she told them that Malaysia was the world's largest tin producer. She noticed the German couple taking photographs and they smiled at her. They had been very pleased at the action she had taken last night after they had been ripped off at the night club they had gone to.

Susan had phoned a highly-placed Malay police officer she knew and within minutes two detectives had arrived and with Susan and the German couple they went back to the night club. The Malaysian police treated offences against tourists very seriously, for tourism was a major source of revenue to the country. The rip-off the German couple had experienced was settled within minutes and they were reimbursed, with abject apologies from the proprietor.

Sitting in her jump seat as they drove on after their stop at the tin-dredging plant, Susan wished her own problems could be solved so simply. Her eyes were red-rimmed from lack of sleep and she was feeling more miserable by the hour. Looking at David's grim face in front of her didn't improve matters, and she thought again of Greg and Tanya somewhere behind in the Mercedes David and she had driven from Singapore.

It had been David's idea that he took Greg's place in the coach. He had said he wanted to talk with Susan, because he had a lot to say to her. She had warned him she wouldn't stand it if he planned to go on reproaching her for last night, but he told her that subject was now closed.

Last night, after the German couple's problem had been dealt with, David had told her what he thought about her 'neglect of her responsibilities'. Although Susan felt he had been pretty fair. He hadn't kept on about it, once she had admitted she had been at fault. He had accepted her explanation that she had had a long day and a long night and could reasonably expect that once her charges were all back in the hotel she was entitled to relax—in whatever way she felt inclined.

That was the part David didn't like—her being in Greg's suite. She told him nothing had happened between Greg and herself and he had looked at her sceptically. She had flared at him, 'If you don't believe me then I don't want to talk to you again— ever!'

He had said hastily that he believed her, although the circumstances he had found her in in Greg's suite had given him, as he put it, 'reasonable cause for doubting her'.

More than reasonable cause, she thought dejectedly. If David had arrived one hour later she mightn't then have been able to protest her innocence. She badly wanted to tell him she was in love with Greg, but she knew it wasn't the moment, especially when he began giving her *his* problems—which were the reason he had made the sudden dash from Singapore to join the tour group in Kuala Lumpur.

David told her that things had come to a head between himself and K.K. Apparently K.K. was negotiating with a wealthy friend who was prepared to provide substantial new capital which Tiger Tours badly needed for new vehicles. K.K. was prepared to put in an equal amount of new capital, but David couldn't match K.K. or the new investor, so he had become a minority stockholder.

Susan queried, 'So why don't you sell out?'

He shook his head. 'Who'd buy a twenty per cent share? Only K.K. or his friend—and they can offer me as little as they want to. But there is one other way——'

'What's that?'

He took a deep breath. 'Well, K.K. is tough, as we know, but he's also very fair. So he's given me an alternative.'

'Which is?' she asked.

'It all hinges on Greg McKenzie. K.K. has said that if we can swing a contract with Greg's Trans Asia Tours, then it would change the whole picture. With a guaranteed contract from T.A.T. it would be like money in the bank. We could borrow the capital we need without having to bring in any outside investor.'

She said slowly, 'I see—so it all depends on Greg.'

David nodded. 'Yes. And luckily, Greg's the

kind of chap who makes up his mind fast. So K.K. thought it was worth me getting up here and joining the tour and spending a couple of days close to Greg. The idea is that I—we—try to sell him on launching a tour programme to this region—using Tiger Tours, naturally.'

'And Tanya,' Susan asked, 'why was she sent with you?'

He coughed. 'Well, K.K. didn't think you and Greg would hit it off too well—remembering how you started off on the wrong foot with him in Singapore.' He averted his eyes. 'K.K. would be pleased to know that he's behind the times, and that you and Greg are now getting along—rather well together.' Then he added hastily, 'Anyway, K.K. thought Tanya might—might be——'

Susan's lips tightened. 'Might be able to—sell the idea to Greg better than I could?'

David coloured. 'Something like that. K.K. was worried that you might rub Greg up the wrong way and kill any chance of a deal. He thought it was worth sending Tanya with me so she could give Greg more—personal attention. The VIP treatment, I mean.'

As she sat in the coach staring at David, Susan recalled her discussion with him last night and reflected bitterly that Tanya was certainly giving Greg her personal attention. He was now getting an individual tour in the company's best limousine, with Tanya as his personal escort and guide.

But she drew some consolation from the fact that Greg hadn't been especially keen about the arrangement that he should follow the coach in the

car with Tanya. But David had mentioned wanting
to discuss company matters with Susan in the
coach, so Greg had agreed to travel with Tanya.
But Susan knew he would have preferred to be with
her.

At the Merlin, following the frustrating interruption of their lovemaking in his suite, she had
barely managed to speak alone with Greg before
they took off in the morning. The brief moment
they had snatched together had been something at
least.

It had been after breakfast in the hotel coffee
shop. Susan had eaten listlessly with David when
they had been joined by Greg and a radiant Tanya,
who, alone among them, looked as if she had
enjoyed a good night's sleep.

Greg was withdrawn and noncommittal during
breakfast and they would have been a morose
foursome if it hadn't been for Tanya, who was
sparkling.

She was wearing a short green dress, slit at the
thigh and cut low at the front. Susan, in her every-
day uniform, felt dowdy beside her. It was over
breakfast that they made the travel arrangements
for the day and Greg agreed to go with Tanya in
the car.

Susan left the table shortly after this and as she
waited glumly for the elevator Greg strode up
behind her and drew her aside.

His expression was sombre as he studied her pale
face and red-rimmed eyes. Then he forced a smile
and commented, 'We're not having much luck, are
we? With your—responsibilities.'

She said dully, 'I *am* working. This is my job.'

Then she tried to brighten up. She was wretchedly aware, after what David had told her, how important Greg now was to Tiger Tours. The knowledge made her feel guilty, as if she was a party to using Greg for business reasons.

She forced a weak smile. 'It looks as if we're never going to be able to have a proper talk together. Not on this tour anyway.'

Greg took her arm and squeezed it. 'We've got tonight in Ipoh. Third time's got to be lucky.'

She sighed. 'Yes, but David—and Tanya—will be there. I don't think I'd have the nerve to come to your room with them around.'

Greg grinned as he squeezed her hand again. 'We'll work something out,' he said confidently. He glanced around, but there were people everywhere. 'I'd like to kiss you,' he said quietly. 'Very much. And tonight I will. But this time there won't be any interruptions.'

Susan smiled wanly. 'I wish I could be certain of that!'

He said earnestly, 'I give you my word that nothing on earth will stop me being with you tonight. Do you believe me?'

Her spirits lifted suddenly. 'Yes. Oh, yes, I do! I'll think about it all day while I'm stuck in the coach with David—and you're in the car with Tanya.'

He smiled. 'Thinking about tonight will keep me going too.'

Sitting in the coach facing David, she knew that the affection she felt for him was nothing compared to the love she felt for Greg. She was certain Greg loved her too, although he hadn't said so yet. But that had hardly been his fault. Anyway, tonight everything should be all right—more than all right. It should be—would be—absolute heaven to hear him say he loved her and to be able to tell him that she loved him.

He had assured her that nothing on earth would keep him away from her, and her heart turned over as she thought of last night and his forceful yet tender wooing. Her lips curved in a smile of remembrance, and, glancing up, she saw that David was smiling at her, assuming her smile was for him. She looked quickly towards the back of the coach and out the rear window to see if Greg and Tanya's car was in sight.

She sighed. And where was her lover right now? Following in the car with another woman—exposed to her provocative sexiness all day long! But still, what did that matter? He had promised that tonight he would be hers.

During the lunch stop at a restaurant in Bidor, Tanya drove up in the car after David and Susan were seated among the passengers, and skilfully steered Greg to the other end of the long table, so Susan had no chance to talk with him.

After lunch they boarded the coach for its final leg to Ipoh, and just past Tapah, Susan drew their attention to the turn-off to the Cameron Highlands. She explained that it was Malaya's most popular hill resort, dating from British colonial days. But they didn't have time to visit it on the tour because the drive up and down the narrow, twisting switchback road would take too long.

Instead, they stopped at an orchid plantation where everybody went mad photographing the colourful and exotic orchids Malaya is famous for.

During the stop, Susan noticed that Tanya and Greg's car didn't catch up with them. Generally it had stayed a few hundred yards behind the coach since leaving Kuala Lumpur. But it hadn't appeared by the time they re-boarded the coach to continue to Ipoh.

David said, 'Tanya probably stopped back on the road to show Greg something. But I'm sure they'll catch up with us soon.'

Susan made no comment as she took her seat and the coach drove off. Munir gave her a sidelong glance as the coach got into high gear. He murmured, *'Ikan gantong kuching tungúu!'*

She smiled wanly at his old-fashioned Malay proverb. Translated, what he had said was, 'The fish is suspended, the cat is waiting.'

After they reached Ipoh and the passengers and baggage had been transferred to their hotel, the Mercedes with Tanya and Greg still hadn't arrived.

David said, 'I shouldn't worry about them. Tanya might have stopped in Tapah for a while. It's an interesting little place.'

Susan didn't reply, but forced a smile. She refused David's offer of a drink and said she wanted to go to her room and do some laundry, as she hadn't managed to do any the night before. But what she really wanted was to get some rest, for she was worn out after her sleepless night in Kuala Lumpur.

In her room she forced herself to rinse out some things and hang them up to dry. Then she staggered to the bed and collapsed wearily. Fortunately, the tour group had a free night in Ipoh, so she had the evening to herself. She decided she could safely sleep for an hour or so, then she would get changed and go down for dinner. No doubt she and Greg would have to share a table with David and Tanya. But later, she would be alone with Greg. She dozed off, dreaming about spending the night in his arms while he told her how much he loved her. Lulled by pleasant thoughts, she fell into a deep sleep until she heard a bell shrilling and threw her head from side to side to block out the sound. Finally she struggled awake, to hear the bedside telephone ringing insistently. She rolled over and dazedly picked up the receiver.

'Hello?' she muttered, then rubbed her eyes as David's voice sounded in her ears.

'Are you coming down for dinner?' he asked. 'It's eight o'clock.'

'Oh, lord! I've been sound asleep. Yes, I—I'll be down. But I may be a while, I've got to have a shower and get dressed.'

'Don't hurry,' he said. 'There'll only be me and you at the table.'

'Oh! Why? What's—I mean, aren't Greg and Tanya joining us?'

David didn't answer for a few seconds and she said, 'Hello? Are you there?'

'Yes,' he said, '*I'm* here. Although they're not.

But they're O.K. I got a call from them a little while ago.'

'Where are they?' she asked dully, gripping the phone.

'In the Cameron Highlands. They detoured up there—but they left it too late to drive back down before the road closed for the night.'

Susan's heart sank and she stared disbelievingly at the phone. She knew—and Tanya knew too—that the narrow mountain road that was the only access to the Highlands was often closed to traffic after dark. Usually this was because of the danger of landslips following heavy tropical rain.

She cried out, 'Why did she take him up there? It's miles off the highway!'

'I don't know. Although she said it's a place Greg ought to see. And I suppose it is—it's quite a contrast with what he's seen so far.'

The Cameron Highlands had originally been where the colonial British vacationed to escape the enervating tropical heat of Malaya. It was a pleasantly cool hill resort, and Susan had been there several times and enjoyed the thrill of sleeping under two blankets again and sitting around a blazing log fire in her lodge. It had been a relief to get away from the constant sticky heat of Singapore and the lowlands.

Now she imagined Tanya and Greg sitting around a fire, drinking hot toddy before retiring for the night. And, she thought anguishedly, Greg wouldn't need blankets to keep warm if Tanya had her way!

David said, 'Hello, Susan—are you still there?'

'Yes,' she mumbled, 'I'm still here.'

He went on, 'And oh, Greg said he'd call you—about this time, in fact. Which is why I thought I'd better wake you.'

'Thanks,' she muttered.

'Are you coming down for dinner?'

'No,' she said numbly. 'I—I don't feel like any.'

His tone was disappointed, but he said he understood. 'You had a late night last night. You need a good sleep. I'll see you in the morning.'

Susan let the receiver drop into its cradle, then sat staring blindly at it. She supposed there was no reason why Tanya shouldn't have taken Greg on a side trip. But why had he agreed to go with her, if he knew they mightn't be able to get to Ipoh that night? Then she thought he probably hadn't realised he could be isolated in the Highlands for the night. That would be something Tanya would have sprung on him!

Dejectedly, she threw herself on the bed and told herself that Greg would phone soon and then everything would be better. But, she thought miserably, whatever he said, he wouldn't be with her tonight, but in a snug mountain lodge with Tanya.

She stared blindly up at a little Malayan gecko which scampered across the ceiling, looking like a miniature dragon with its flicking tongue. Geckos could hang on to anything, even when they were upside down. She thought about her fragile love affair, which was all topsy-turvy after this latest blow. But like the gecko, she would have to try and cling to what little she had.

She lay for an hour, trying not to think of Greg with Tanya and telling herself that she must fight the jealousy and anger that was mounting within her. But still the phone didn't ring, no matter how much she willed it to do so.

Finally she got up and put on her nightdress, then got into bed, burying her face miserably in the pillow.

Another hour crawled past and she told herself that she didn't care now if he didn't ring. He's said he would ring over two hours ago—but he hadn't. He hadn't even tried. Obviously he'd become too caught up in whatever he and Tanya were doing. It was impossible that he had any real feelings for her, or he would never have left her like this— waiting, and hoping every minute for his call. She beat her fist against the pillow and told herself she would scornfully refuse to take his call when—and if—it came through tonight.

An hour later the phone rang, and as she snatched it up she glanced at her watch and saw it was after eleven.

In spite of her resentment, Greg's voice sounded like music in her ears, and her heart lifted slightly.

'Hi, Susan,' he said. 'Sorry I couldn't call earlier. We got into a party, with some visiting American travel agents. You know what they're like?'

'Yes,' she said, trying to control her ill humour. She did know what groups of travel agents were like when they were on a junket trip. It was one long party every night. But she supposed Greg had to be nice to them, because they sold his company's tours.

'I just made it back to my room,' he went on, 'so I'm relaxing.'

'And Tanya,' she said evenly, 'how is she?'

'Oh, you know—she was the life and soul of the party. The star attraction.'

'She always is. I expect the travel agents were all men?'

'Yes, they were.'

In the background Susan suddenly heard Tanya's voice calling out, and her grip on the phone tightened. She asked tautly, 'Tanya is with you?'

'Yes. She said to say hello to you.'

'Thank you,' said Susan, trying to control her rising fury. 'I'm glad you're now able to relax.'

Greg's voice dropped a tone. 'Look, Susan, I'll tell you all about everything tomorrow. We're planning an early start and we should be in Ipoh around the time you leave for Khedar. If we miss you, we'll catch up fast. Tanya knows your route backwards.'

'I know she does. She's been at this game longer than I have. I'm sure you'll be in good hands.'

His tone was low but placating. 'I can't talk much right now. But hang on until tomorrow, huh?'

Susan's grip on the receiver tightened. 'I have no intention of hanging on!' she said tartly. 'Not until tomorrow—and not on this phone either—not while you—you—*relax* up there with *her*!'

'Look, Susan,' he said soothingly, 'don't blow your top! Just wait until I'm with you, then we'll——' He broke off and she heard Tanya calling out.

Greg said, 'Hold on, Susan—Tanya's got something she wants to tell you. No, wait, she wants to have a word with you ...'

Susan snapped into the phone, 'But I don't want to speak to her! You can tell her to—to go to hell!'

'Come on, Susan,' he protested, 'stay cool. I'll tell her you're too tired to talk any more.'

'I *am* too tired to talk any more!' she cried. 'To her—and to you too! You can—oh! You can——'

She heard his voice, distant over the wire, as he said coldly, 'You mean I can go to hell too?'

'Yes!' she snapped. 'And don't hurry to catch up with us. I'd rather not see you again!'

His voice came harshly. 'That won't be hard to organise! I won't follow you tomorrow—I'll get Tanya to drive me straight through to Penang. Goodbye, Miss York!'

CHAPTER EIGHT

NEXT morning it rained heavily, and the depressing tropical downpour matched Susan's dismal spirits. It was Day Four of the tour and usually it was the high spot of the trip. Most of the day—and the night—would be spent at Sultan Khedar's palace. Few tour groups got the opportunity of experiencing palace life, as Jimmy had given David's company exclusive rights to bring tourists to the historic old royal residence.

On the short drive from Ipoh to Khedar Palace, the passengers' spirits weren't dampened by the lashing rain, which stopped abruptly half an hour after they left Ipoh. The tourists had by this time got to know each other, and during their hours in the coach they exchanged a lot of goodnatured banter.

Susan thought they had been a really good group and she had relatively few problems with them. The few she had had—Maimie's tummy upset and the German couple being ripped off—had only been problems because of her own intense involvement with Greg on both occasions. If he hadn't been on the tour with her then she would have considered it a pretty smooth trip so far.

With a great effort of will she pushed thoughts of Greg from her mind and concentrated on thinking about her passengers. She didn't want to think about him and add more pain to her aching heart. Thank goodness she had had a nice bunch of people on the coach with her and none of the nasties who could make a tour difficult.

Sometimes, many passengers seemed intent on complaining about everything, and she wondered why they bothered to take the fairly expensive tour at all. Others passed the time squabbling with their spouses, which made it hard for fellow passengers, and especially for Susan, whose job it was to make sure everybody enjoyed their tour.

Occasionally, too, she had to suffer smart alecks, or compulsive wisecrackers. Other pests were loud-mouthed 'experienced' travellers, who insisted on giving their own commentary while she was explaining points of interest. But on this trip, the group had all been very pleasant and well-behaved, and they had been highly-cooperative, which was one of the things that helped make a smooth, happy tour.

She thought about the beginning of the tour, with Greg close to her all day. It had really been rather wonderful, and she looked back on the first two days almost nostalgically. It had been a very arousing and warmly exciting forty-eight hours. And it had been blissfully uncomplicated—until David and Tanya arrived, when everything started going wrong.

At the rear of the coach, some passengers began singing and David patted the vacant seat alongside himself and signalled for Susan to join him. She left the jump seat reluctantly. She didn't really want to talk to him, but while the passengers were singing she couldn't interrupt with commentary, so she got up and sat stiffly beside him.

He coughed, then asked if Greg had phoned her last night. She said shortly that he had, but she didn't tell him anything Greg had said to her, or his bitter parting words. She assumed Tanya would contact David at Khedar Palace and tell him she would be driving Greg straight through to Penang. She didn't know what David would think about that, and she didn't care.

Finally, David said tentatively, 'I'm a bit annoyed with Tanya—taking Greg up to the Camerons and getting stranded with him last night. But——' he hesitated, then went on, 'perhaps it's a good thing.' He coughed, then added, 'Business-wise, I mean.'

Susan glanced at him bleakly. 'You mean she's had plenty of opportunity to butter him up—and squeeze some business out of him—for you!'

He flushed under her withering gaze.

She went on, her cheeks flaming, 'I think it's—disgusting! And both you and K.K. should be ashamed of yourselves!'

David said defensively, 'I'm not too happy about it. But I don't think for a moment that Tanya's wiles will influence Greg in our favour. He's too good a businessman. If he decides to start tours to this region it'll be based on what he thinks of the attractions of the area—and cold hard factors like what price we can offer so he can make a profit. And that's where I come in—let's hope, tonight at the palace.'

She was silent. David was going to be very upset

when he found Greg wouldn't be staying with them at the palace tonight. Which was really her fault, she supposed. She grimaced. She'd really made a mess of everything—her love affair, and David's business affairs.

The passengers stopped their community singing as Munir steered the coach off the main highway on to the road to Khedar Palace. Luke Eikhorn asked her about Malaysian royalty and she explained that the nation was a constitutional monarchy, ruled by a *Yang*, or king, who must always be one of the Sultans from nine of the thirteen States in the Federation which still had Sultans.

She told him that the Sultanate of Khedar was a very old one, although the Sultan's son Jimmy was very progressive. He was also very internationally-minded and was anxious to show selected groups of foreign visitors what life was like in a palace in a modern democracy. Jimmy's father had been dubious about opening up the palace to tourists, but he had finally given his son *carte blanche* to make suitable arrangements to accommodate small groups and entertain them for a twenty-four-hour stay.

When they arrived at the palace gates, two smartly-uniformed Malay sentries sprang to attention and the sergeant of the guard saluted, then waved the coach on. At the palace, the major-domo efficiently organised a platoon of servants to carry the baggage and show the guests to their accommodation.

The palace was a sprawling, two-story building

of stone and timber construction, mainly heavy teak and mahogany. It was built around a large central courtyard which was dotted with fountains and pools set amongst beautiful garden beds and lawns.

One side of the top floor of the palace had been the original harem wing, where the many wives of earlier Sultans had lived with their children and servants. Most of the rooms in the harem wing had balconies which looked down into the courtyard. The balconies had been covered by heavy, slatted timber shutters so the women could see out but nobody could see in.

Jimmy had raised the shutters for the first time in two centuries and converted the harem wing into visitor accommodation. He had retained the traditional Eastern decor and most of the old furniture and drapes, but he'd added modern amenities, like bathrooms.

The rooms were a mixture. Some, which had been used by the wives, were large, while others were very small, having been for the servants. Susan, being on her own, was given one of the smaller rooms and David got a larger one next door to her. She assumed the tactful proximity of their rooms had been decided by Jimmy, who personally oversaw all the arrangements for his guests.

But Susan didn't mind her tiny room, for it was more important that the clients got the larger ones.

The tourists loved the experience of sleeping the night in a former harem and the opportunity to see how Malay royalty lived. Jimmy threw open most of the palace to them except for the wing where he and his family lived.

In the three months since the palace had been included in the tours, everything had gone well and the visitors had respected the fact that they were staying at a family home as well as a historic old palace. The Sultan had grudgingly admitted that Jimmy's idea had been a good one, for visitors usually went away with a much better appreciation of the life led by modern Malay rulers.

Susan's group arrived in time for morning tea, which they were served on one of the cool terraces looking out over sweeping lawns which had been cultivated like an English park. Jimmy welcomed them on behalf of his father, who was away in Penang with Jimmy's English mother.

After tea, he escorted the group round his pride and joy—a big museum he had created featuring early horse-drawn vehicles and carriages, many of which had been used by his ancestors on cere-monial occasions since the eighteenth century.

Susan was left with very little to do, for Jimmy enthusiastically took over her role as tour guide, so she was virtually free until lunchtime.

Munir also wasn't required until next morning, so he took the opportunity to visit his home village, which was only a few miles away and which the tour group would lunch at next day as a side trip on their final run to Penang. David drove with Munir in the coach to Munir's village so that he could bring the coach back to the palace.

After Jimmy had taken the tour group to his transport museum and David had driven off in the coach, Susan was left very much on her own and she thought bitterly about Greg, who had now disappeared out of her life for ever. With an aching heart she remembered what he had said last time she had seen him in Kuala Lumpur—'I give you my word that nothing on earth will stop me being with you tonight.'

Well, she thought savagely, it hadn't taken much to keep him from her! Just a simple ploy by Tanya and he'd fallen for it. And spent the night at a drunken travel agents' party—then taken Tanya back to his room! She told herself she was well rid of him. Obviously he had only been playing with her, seeking company for his bed during their stopovers. But he had found too many frustrations trying to win her, so, the moment Tanya turned up, he had switched to her and it was goodbye, Miss York!

Susan wished fervently that this miserable tour would end so she could get back to Singapore and work out what she was going to do with her life now her dreams of love had been shattered. She couldn't see herself staying in the East—certainly not at Tiger Tours with Tanya gloating over her every time they met.

She thought miserably that now it was all over with Greg she had better start putting him out of her mind and thinking about her future. One thing was certain, after this tour she was going to leave Singapore and get as far away from the East as possible.

Canada seemed the best place to go, as she had an aunt in Vancouver—her father's sister, whom she liked, although she hadn't seen her for years. But then, she reflected, Vancouver was a little too close to Los Angeles, where Greg lived. And she wouldn't want to see him again!

She went for a walk through the beautifully-tended grounds of the palace. The old building stood in several hundred acres, surrounded by a high stone wall that ran for miles. She walked along the main driveway, which was as wide as a regular road, and lined by every type of tropical tree and flowering shrub.

At the main gate the two uniformed sentries saluted her, and she smiled at them, then turned and walked back the way she had come. When she reached the palace, David drove up in the coach, and she waited while he drove it out of sight into a parking lot surrounded by trees.

They made forced conversation for a few minutes, then David said, 'I wonder what's keeping Tanya? They should have been here by now.'

Susan said shortly, 'I don't think she will be. I think Greg wants to go straight to Penang, so she's probably taking him there.'

David frowned. 'She wouldn't do that without telling me. I mean, I want to see Greg—that's the reason I'm up here.' Then suddenly his face cleared and he pointed down the drive. 'No, you're wrong. Here they are now!'

Susan wheeled and saw the Mercedes coming up the drive. As it approached, she saw Greg in the passenger seat beside Tanya. She said quickly, her face flaming, 'I—I must go and join the others. Jimmy will need me.' She turned and ran towards the palace.

She hurried up to her tiny room and paced up and down distractedly. She had only had the briefest glimpse of Greg in the car, but it had been enough to upset her. She just couldn't have faced him, especially not with Tanya there, gloating.

She guessed that Tanya had called in on their way to Penang to tell David what was happening. No doubt they'd then leave. Soon, she hoped, because she couldn't stay hiding in her room for ever. She would have to attend lunch for the tourists as Jimmy would be expecting her. Usually she sat with him at meal times.

She stayed in her room for nearly an hour, when she decided she would have to go down to the terrace where lunch would be served. As she left her room she almost walked into Tanya, who was followed by a Malay servant carrying her suitcase.

Tanya was wearing a short yellow cotton dress with a Chinese collar and bell sleeves. It was unbuttoned revealingly at the neck. She looked weary, but happy. And fulfilled, Susan thought bitterly.

She looked languidly at Susan and said, 'Hello, Suzy.' She nodded to the servant, who bowed and squeezed past them.

Susan said shortly, 'So you're staying. I thought you might be going on to Penang.'

Tanya smiled. 'No—Greg decided he wanted to see the palace.' She smiled archly. 'And did you have a good night in Ipoh?'

Susan's lips tightened. 'You mean you want me to ask if you had a good night in the Camerons?'

Tanya smiled. 'It was a wonderful night!' She

rolled her eyes and moistened her lips suggestively. 'What a man! He's incredibly virile!'

Susan struggled to control herself. 'Oh, shut up!' she blurted out inadequately. 'I—I detest you!'

'Tut, tut,' Tanya drawled, her smile widening. 'That's not like the ladylike Miss York, is it?'

Susan made to push past her. 'I may just forget I'm a lady,' she snapped, 'if I talk to you any more!'

Tanya caught her arm and her face became vicious. Susan knew there had never been any love lost between them, but she was surprised at the venom in the other girl's eyes as she glared at her.

'You've always had David!' she said accusingly. 'All to yourself. But you can't have all the men, you know! And you certainly won't have Greg— not now he's had me!'

Susan's face flamed and she choked on the anguish that rose in her throat. She tried to think of something adequate to say, but nothing was good enough—or bad enough. Instead, she stared at Tanya's taunting face, then swung on her heel and strode blindly down the corridor. She ran downstairs, then out of the building and across the drive towards the parking lot where the coach stood behind some trees.

She opened the door and stumbled up the steps, then went to the rear seats and threw herself down. Well, she scolded herself, fighting back tears, what did you expect? That they'd sit and hold hands all night? Greg might—just might—have been content with that, but there was no way Tanya would have stopped there. And, Susan thought bitterly, as I well know, Greg is a very virile male.

She forced herself to keep her eyes wide open and sat staring, refusing to blink or that would have released the tears. She was damned if she'd cry over him!

Then up front she heard the coach door open, and quickly swung herself into a sitting position as she saw Greg striding purposefully along the aisle towards her.

She jumped to her feet and began to move towards him, but he reached her in a few strides and grabbed her by the shoulders, thrusting her back into the seat. He sat down beside her, holding her with one arm while she writhed and struggled furiously.

'Cut it out!' he commanded. 'You're not leaving. We're going to have a talk.'

'Don't touch me!' she cried, pulling away from him in disgust. 'You've come straight from—being with her—and you've got the nerve to touch me!'

He gave her a little shake. 'What's Tanya been telling you?'

His brow was dark as he stared into her eyes which flared back at him in anger.

'What do you think!' she spat out. 'She was very pleased with herself. And she thought you were wonderful!'

He shook her slightly. 'I think you should listen to me before you go off at half-cock!' He slid one arm around her, but Susan brushed it aside and strained away from him.

Her eyes spat fire as she snapped, 'I prefer to believe her! You see, I know what she's like.

And——' she stared at him, her breasts heaving, 'I know what you're like too!'

Greg's face turned to ice. He jerked away and gazed at her coldly. 'Playtime's over!' he snapped. 'You've got things off your chest—or you should have! But don't ever say you don't believe me. I never have, and never will, lie to you!'

His eyes were smouldering coals of fire as they burned into hers. She felt herself wavering as she lowered her eyes and muttered, 'I don't understand why you couldn't get back last night. You could have, if you'd really wanted to.'

'I couldn't!' he snapped impatiently. 'The road was closed and that was it. There's no helicopter service, no mules—nothing. If I'd started walking down I'd still be walking! But in any case, nothing happened between Tanya and me last night.'

'Huh!' she snorted.

His eyes glinted dangerously. 'I'm only going to say this once. I've told you nothing happened between us—not that it couldn't have, quite easily. But I had you on my mind all night. I didn't want anybody else.'

Susan closed her lips tightly and glared at him.

'Right!' he growled, 'Do you accept my word that nothing happened between us?'

She avoided his eyes and he gave her a vigorous shake.

'Come on!' he snapped. 'A simple yes or no!'

'I—I——' she refused to meet his eyes. 'I don't know. I suppose I have to. But I——'

He leapt to his feet. 'But nothing!' he thundered. 'No reservations! You either believe me or you don't. And when you say you believe me, you could think about apologising for doubting me in the first place.'

She gaped at him. 'Apologise?' she stuttered. 'I haven't even decided whether to forgive you for last night! And you think I should apologise? Oh!'

She jumped to her feet and faced him, staring up at him as he stood with his head slightly bent to avoid hitting the roof of the coach.

She said, quivering with emotion, 'You're the one who should apologise! I spent a dreadful night wondering about you!'

Greg shook his head slowly as he stared at her flushed determined face. He said harshly, 'I think we should forget the whole deal! If there's no trust between us, then going on would be a mistake. So I guess I'll cut my losses and get out of your life now!' He looked at her with bitter scorn.

'You haven't *been* in my life!' she cried. 'You've only tried to—use me! You've never said you loved me!'

A sardonic smile played over his face. 'Wasn't I lucky?' he growled. 'I just stopped short of making an idiot of myself!'

He turned and strode down the aisle and out of the coach.

CHAPTER NINE

THE ornate, high-ceilinged banqueting hall in Khedar Palace resounded with applause as Susan's passengers showed their appreciation of the entertainment that had just ended. They had been watching a programme of traditional Malay dances performed by palace servants, and everyone agreed that the show had been highly professional.

Seated at the head of the long banqueting table, Jimmy looked quietly pleased by the applause, for developing the dance troupe had been another of his pet projects. Susan sat on Jimmy's left and he had placed Greg, as a VIP in the travel industry, on his right. Tanya was beside Greg and she faced David, who was beside Susan.

Susan had been appalled at the seating arrangement, but she had had no choice, for Jimmy insisted she sat beside him, as she always did. But she hadn't bargained on Greg and Tanya being present. She had been sure that after seeing the palace, he meant to go on to Penang and spend the night there with Tanya. But Jimmy had indicated during the day that he would be extremely offended if Greg left the palace without accepting his hospitality for one night. So Greg had stayed, and Jimmy had placed him in a two-roomed suite which had been occupied by the number one wife of earlier Sultans.

After Greg stalked out of the coach, Susan had pulled herself together and joined the tour group for lunch on the terrace. In the afternoon she had helped Jimmy show them around the palace and its grounds. Greg and Tanya hadn't joined them for lunch and Susan assumed she had taken Greg for a drive in the car to show him some of the nearby sights. That would be her excuse anyway, to get him alone, she thought bitterly.

During the afternoon, Jimmy showed the tourists his father's small zoo, which featured many native Malayan animals ranging from tigers to monkeys, but all roaming in an environment as close to nature as possible.

They also visited the Sultan's orchid display, which was one of the best in Malaysia. Then, as the *pièce de résistance,* they were given a conducted tour of the palace. Many rooms were more like museum displays than living areas, and the whole history of North Malaya was contained under their lofty ceilings.

It was nearly dusk when the palace tour finished and the tourists went off to their rooms to change for dinner and the entertainment.

During dinner, Jimmy was in good form. He obviously relished having foreign visitors, for life at the palace could be very isolated for him after his years in England at university.

He was interested in what he called the orderly development of tourism in Malaysia, and he told Greg that many Malays were concerned that the less desirable type of Westerner didn't overrun the country.

Susan knew what he meant. But she also knew it was almost impossible for a white person to 'go native' in places like Singapore or Malaysia. A few hippies from Western countries had tried it over the years, but the government wouldn't permit it. Unless visitors had adequate—and visible—means of support, they were quickly escorted out of the country. Basically, the government didn't want radical young Westerners infecting their own people with what they called 'advanced' ideas. This was especially so in Malaysia, a Muslim nation, which clung to traditional Muslim beliefs and customs.

Jimmy, David and Greg discussed this, but Susan took little part in the debate. Jimmy glanced at her once or twice, his expression quizzical. Normally at the palace she was a bright conversationalist and she usually kept Jimmy entertained with a lot of badinage such as he had been used to during his university days. But she was painfully aware of Greg opposite her and how he avoided looking at her or talking directly to her, although he conversed freely with everyone else.

She was thankful when the *gamelan* music began and the entertainment started. Then, after the show, the traditional music was replaced by a modern four-piece dance band, and Jimmy invited everybody to get up and dance. He claimed Susan for the first dance, and Greg danced with Tanya while David invited Maimie Eikhorn on to the floor. Most of the rest of the group also danced, and it became quite a swinging night.

During dinner they had been served champagne,

but although his father was absent, Jimmy didn't over-indulge. He took his duties as host very seriously.

After an hour's dancing, he signalled the band leader to take a break and coffee was served.

Maimie Eikhorn, who was sitting one down from Susan, on the other side of David, leaned forward and raised her glass to Jimmy and said, 'We've got to thank you for a really swell time, Your Highness. It's been the best day of the tour, and Luke and I have enjoyed it more than anything we've seen so far.'

Jimmy smiled. He'd asked everyone, including Maimie, to call him Jimmy, but she insisted on giving him his title. He raised his glass and said, 'I'm glad you've enjoyed it, Mrs Eikhorn. We have many interesting things here at the Palace, and I've always believed we shouldn't keep them locked up to be seen only by the family. I like to think we are sharing our heritage with our own people—and with people from other lands.'

Luke Eikhorn said, 'We'll never stop talking about this when we get home. Maimie won't anyway. We've seen a few palaces in Europe, but nobody lives in them any more. This has been a great experience.'

Jimmy smiled. 'Thank you. And now I must propose a toast to that much-maligned species, the American tourist.' He raised his glass and toasted the Eikhorns who flushed with pleasure.

When conversation become general, Jimmy said to Greg and Susan, 'Touring is supposed to be relaxing, but I think it's really hard work. I do admire middle-aged people like the Eikhorns. They have a lot of stamina.'

Susan nodded. 'They're really quite remarkable. You can keep them on the go from dawn to dusk, even in sticky heat like Malaya's. You can steer them in and out of mosques, up and down temple stairs, around market places, into jungle villages, and they don't mind how hard you push them so long as they see everything—and photograph it all.'

Greg said, 'Provided he has an air-conditioned room to come back to at nights, the Yankee tourist is a very hardy breed.'

Susan glanced covertly at him. He hadn't looked at her when he'd spoken, but at least he had acknowledged that she was there and sitting opposite him. Until then, he hadn't *completely* ignored her, but when he had looked at her his expression had been cold and remote.

She was glad she hadn't bothered to dress up for the occasion. Jimmy had in any case told everyone to dress informally, as he knew the tourists wouldn't carry evening dress with them. He set the standard by wearing a casual white jacket with an open-necked shirt. Greg and David were also dressed in white tropical jackets with casual shirts.

Susan wore a full cotton skirt in a bright print, topped by a cream silk shirt with gathered yoke and cuffed sleeves. Next to Greg, Tanya was in an exquisitely embroidered cheong-sam, slit high on both sides, her dark hair in a gleaming coil on top of her head.

Greg said, 'I'm glad you pressed me to stay,

Jimmy, or I'd have missed something really worth while. In fact, this visit to your home has helped me decide to launch a tour programme to Malaysia.'

Beside Susan, David started and she glanced at him and saw his face break into a smile. He said quickly, 'You'll avail yourself of our services for the land arrangements, I hope?'

Greg nodded. 'I surely will. I've been very impressed with your operations.' He glanced at Tanya beside him. 'Your tour conductors are good. They go out of their way to give your clients personal attention. I hope my clients will get the same treatment.'

David nodded vigorously. 'They will! They will! You can depend on that.'

Greg said to Jimmy, 'I'd like to think that the tour groups I send will be able to experience this visit to the palace. Would you feel inclined to receive them?'

Jimmy asked, 'How many people will you be sending?'

Greg said, 'To begin with, only about thirty each week.'

Jimmy nodded. 'I'd be happy to have them. With David's regular tour that means we'd receive two groups a week. I think we can handle that without disrupting palace life.'

'Fine,' Greg smiled. 'I'm delighted.'

'And so am I,' said Jimmy. 'If visiting the palace helps bring more Americans to Malaysia then it will benefit the entire country.'

'And I'm delighted too,' David said, beaming.

Tanya smiled. 'Everyone's delighted,' she commented. 'And I am too—for Greg is going to take me on as a guide for Trans Asia Tours.'

Susan stared at her. Greg nodded and looked at David. 'Yes, we talked about it last night at the Cameron Highlands. I'm sorry to poach her from you, David. But with Tanya's knowledge of the East, she'll be an asset to us.'

David said, 'Well, yes, we'll be sorry to lose Tanya. Will she be based here, or in America?'

'In Los Angeles,' said Greg. 'But she'll spend most of her time taking our groups around Asia. The number of languages she speaks makes her very valuable to us.'

'Well, congratulations!' David said to Tanya, 'and I'm sure Greg will pay you more than you get with us.'

Tanya smiled. 'Much more.' She stroked Greg's arm. 'And there are all kinds of fringe benefits.'

Susan felt ill. Jimmy raised his glass and said, 'Well, everybody seems to have something to celebrate. So let's drink to—to the future.'

Keeping her eyes resolutely on the table, Susan raised her glass and touched it to her lips. The band struck up a modern waltz and David got to his feet and took Susan's arm and said, 'May I have this dance?'

The last thing she felt like was dancing, but she didn't want to stay at the table either and look at Tanya's glowing face—or Greg's face as he smiled at her.

On the floor, David hugged Susan and said, 'And that solves all my problems! Even only one tour a week from Greg changes the whole picture for Tiger Tours. And if we look after his people well, then who knows how business from him could grow!'

He was so excited he almost began doing a polka, which was awkward for her as the band was playing a waltz.

Susan let herself be whirled around the floor. She didn't trust herself to speak. But David was so excited he didn't notice her silence as he babbled on about how wonderfully everything had turned out. Then the music changed to a slower number and David drew her close and whispered, 'This will make a lot of difference to the future—our future. In a couple of years Tiger Tours will be quite a large business and I'd have no difficulty selling my share for a good price.' He mumbled something against her shoulder. He lowered his head and murmured into her ear, 'There's really nothing to prevent us getting married now—and soon.'

She muttered that she'd think about it after the tour was over, and he kissed her cheek as they glided round the floor.

Finally she said she had had enough dancing and he led her back to the table where he promptly claimed Tanya, telling her he wanted to talk to her about her new job. At the same time, Maimie Eikhorn came up and boldly asked Jimmy for a dance. At the top end of the table, Susan was left alone facing Greg.

She picked up her bag, stood up and said, 'Excuse me.' But he reached over and took her hand and asked her to sit down.

She avoided his eyes, two spots of colour burning on her cheeks. 'I was going to the powder room,' she lied.

He shook his head. 'No, I think you were going to your bedroom. What's the matter—don't you like seeing people being happy?'

Susan flopped down into her chair and looked at him defiantly. 'Yes, I like seeing people happy. You've made *everyone* very happy tonight—David, Jimmy and Tanya.'

He grinned suddenly. 'But not Susan! Don't you like the idea of Tanya working for me?'

She tossed her head. 'It's a matter of complete indifference to me who works for you!'

He smiled. 'I could hardly offer *you* the job. I mean you've got David to think of, then also, you don't speak as many languages as Tanya—and of course, our personal relationship would have made our working together impossible.'

She gaped at him. 'Personal relationship? What personal relationship? Some kisses, some sweet talk, a broken promise—and some lies! I don't call that a relationship!'

'It might have been,' he drawled, 'if you'd given it a chance—and trusted me.'

'Trust you! How could I trust you? You swore nothing would keep you away from me last night—and what happened?'

He looked bored. 'I don't propose to go into that again. It's a waste of time trying to talk sense to a jealous woman.'

'Jealous!' she exclaimed. 'Why should I be jealous?'

He grinned. 'You know exactly why. But you won't admit it.'

She stared at him. 'You think I'm—was in love with you? Oh! You really are conceited!'

She snatched her bag and jumped to her feet, but Greg rose and came quickly round the table and caught her arm. The music changed to a slow foxtrot. 'Let's dance,' he said.

Susan pulled her arm away and stood facing him, quivering with fury. Jimmy came back to the table and held out the chair for Maimie Eikhorn.

He glanced quickly at Susan and Greg, then said, 'You know the village is having a traditional wedding tomorrow, Greg, and everyone's invited. I hope you'll stay on for it.'

Greg nodded as Jimmy walked back to his chair. 'I might stay for it,' he said. 'I might as well see this tour through to the end.'

Jimmy said, 'I expect you get tired of seeing traditional Malay weddings, Susan. They can become very boring.'

Greg said, 'I don't think women ever find weddings boring. Even when they're not the bride.'

Jimmy nodded, 'Our Malay wedding ceremony is really rather pleasant. Don't you agree, Susan?'

Both men looked at her as she stood staring at Greg, her face flaming. She choked back a retort and managed to say evenly, 'Yes, Jimmy, they are pleasant. But I agree with you that they can become boring. So I may pass up tomorrow's. I really don't think I could take it.'

She nodded politely to him. 'If you'll excuse me, please, Jimmy. I'm feeling very tired.'

She turned on her heel, ignoring Greg, and marched out of the hall.

CHAPTER TEN

AFTER she had hurried out of the banqueting hall, Susan couldn't face going up to her tiny room. It was still quite early and she knew if she tried to sleep now she would only toss and turn all night on her narrow bed. She was also afraid she might break down and have a good cry, which meant that David might hear her through the thin walls that separated their rooms.

Instead of going up to the harem wing, she ran out of the palace and along the broad pathway that led to the Sultan's zoo. The animals were all on one side of the path and the other side was lightly-wooded parkland, with occasional rustic benches set here and there on the velvety lawns. Above, a full tropical moon made silvery patterns through the trees, bathing the exotic flowers in a shimmering glow.

It was a beautifully romantic scene and the night was warm and balmy. It was an evening—and a setting—made for love, she thought forlornly as she wandered aimlessly across the sweeping lawns.

And what of the man she loved—correction, the man she had thought she loved? He had really tried to hurt her and humiliate her in front of everyone. The way he had let Tanya announce that he was taking her back to America to work for his company. And Tanya talking about fringe benefits while she stroked his arm! So that was what they'd discussed at the Cameron Highlands last night. Taking Tanya to Los Angeles as his employee—and his mistress, obviously.

Then, when he had finally deigned to talk to her, after they had been left alone at the table, he had accused her of being jealous. And he had arrogantly implied that she was in love with him!

Suddenly, miserably, Susen knew he was right on both counts. She *was* bitterly jealous—and she was in love with him.

But after tonight she knew he felt nothing for her. If he had even the slightest feeling for her he could never have behaved as he had done during dinner. He had gone out of his way to show how he had the power to make everyone happy—everyone except her. Jimmy, David, Tanya—they had all been pleased with what he had decided to do. But Susan—she had been dismissed with a wave of his hand because of—their personal relationship. What a joke!

She sank on to a bench under a rubber tree and stared up at the moon. How cruel he was! After their bitter scene in the coach before lunch he had said he had almost made a fool of himself over her. Yet the night before, in the Camerons, he had arranged to take Tanya back to America with him. No, she was the one who had made a fool of herself over him. Everyone knew it, even Munir. And David was aware of it too.

She thought about David and realised she had failed to appreciate what a good man he was. Even after finding her in Greg's suite in Kuala Lumpur, he hadn't berated her. Instead, tonight he had again talked about marrying her. So he had remained steadfast, even while she had thrown herself, infatuated, at another man.

She felt a sudden rush of sympathy for him. They had been good friends since they had met in London and David had offered her the glamorous-sounding Tiger Tours job. He had paid her fare to fly out to Singapore, and he had found her an apartment—no easy task in a city chronically short of accommodation. He had also seen that salary-wise she was well treated, when allowances were added to her basic pay. As their relationship had developed, he had given her a lot of special consideration.

Then through the trees, from the direction of the palace, she saw a white-jacketed figure strolling towards her. Her heart lifted slightly. Good old reliable David! When he had found she had gone he must have decided to follow her. Well, she could do a lot worse than David, and if he wanted to talk about marriage under the full moon, she wouldn't try and stop him.

She peered at the striding figure approaching, then with a leap of her heart she saw it wasn't David, but Greg!

She leapt to her feet in mingled panic and rage, then turned and ran. Behind her, she heard him call, 'Hey, Susan—hold on!'

Clutching her bag, she ran into a grove of trees and weaved and dodged her way round them, looking for a hiding place as she heard his pounding feet racing after her.

She didn't get very far. She was hampered by her high heels and he overtook her within seconds and she felt his hands on her shoulders. She struggled violently as he pulled her to a halt, then swung her round to face him.

'Go away!' she cried breathlessly. 'I don't want to see you or have anything to do with you. I hate and despise you! I don't——'

She closed her mouth suddenly as he gripped her hair and turned her head up and lowered his face to kiss her. She squirmed, but couldn't break free of his grasp, and she had to suffer his mouth covering hers while he pulled her hard against his body. But she refused to let her lips part as he kissed her, although the force and intensity of the contact was such that she could hardly breathe.

Finally she was forced to open her mouth to gulp air, and Greg let her take one gasping breath, then his lips closed over hers again and she was forced to yield and let him kiss her properly. But she refused to let her body display the slightest reaction to his kissing, but let herself hang in his arms, breathing shallowly.

Finally he took his lips away and let her jerk herself back. But he held her, a hand on each of her shoulders, preventing her from escaping.

She panted as she glared up at him. 'All right, you've proved you're bigger and stronger than me. And after tonight, you've proved you're a beast and a rat—and a pig! What more do you want to do?'

He grinned down at her. 'Get you to admit you love me.'

'Oh!' She struggled in his grip. 'Love you? I can't stand you!'

'That wasn't the impression I got in Kuala Lumpur and Malacca.'

'All right!' she snapped. 'So I *was* infatuated with you. That was when I thought you were different from how you really are. But my first impression was right. You're just an arrogant boor! I could never love you.'

He smiled. 'You could try.'

She stamped her foot and trod on his toes. She smiled with satisfaction as she saw him wince.

'You don't know what love is!' she cried. Then to her chagrin, her voice broke. 'You—you were very cruel to me tonight. I—I——'

She let her head hang, and Greg drew her closer and she didn't resist as he gently tilted her chin then kissed her.

Then he took his lips away and said softly, 'I'm sorry, I know I was a brute. But I didn't mean for Tanya to tell everyone she was coming to work for my company. But once she announced it, there was nothing I could do about it.'

'I'm *glad* she announced it,' Susan choked, her face twisting as she tried to look glad.

He smiled. 'I would have told you—eventually. But today, in the coach, didn't seem the time. Last night, in the Camerons, what Tanya and I discussed mainly was her coming to work for us.'

'You mean coming to work for you!' she shot out.

He grinned and said patiently, 'I have a hundred and fifty people working for me. More than half of them are females—and many are every bit as attractive as Tanya.'

'Huh!' she snorted. 'You must have quite a harem to select from, if you keep recruiting them from all around the world every time you travel.'

Greg shook his head. 'I follow the old rule—never fish in the company pond. Once Tanya goes on the payroll, then she's not likely to be bothered by me for any personal reasons.'

'But she's not on your payroll yet, is she?'

He gave her a little shake. 'Susan, I wish you'd stop being jealous about Tanya. I really find you much more attractive than her. And I'll tell you once again, I'm sorry I behaved like I did tonight. But I was very angry with you. Maybe more annoyed than angry.'

'Then you know how I feel!' she shot at him.

Greg said patiently, 'You don't seem to realise how frustrating it was for me last night when I was trapped in the bloody mountains and couldn't get to Ipoh to be with you. You're so wrapped up in your own frustration that you haven't given one thought to the fact that it was a bad night for me too. I wanted very badly to be with you.'

He bent his head and kissed her gently, his lips tentatively probing hers, his arms drawing her close.

She felt herself wavering. 'Were you really annoyed that you couldn't get down the mountain?'

He sighed. 'I was mad with frustration! I came close to blasting the hell out of Tanya, but she claimed the road closing at dusk was a surprise to her. I still don't know if she caused me to be marooned there deliberately. But I gave her the benefit of the doubt.'

Susan said shakily, 'So I suppose I'd better do the same, and give you the benefit of the doubt about her.'

His lips tightened, then relaxed again. 'No,' he said, patiently, 'you don't do that. For as I told you in the coach today, nothing will be any good between us if you have any doubts about me. So— it's up to you.'

She stared up at his face in the moonlight, then she gave a long shuddering sigh and let her head fall against his shoulder. 'No,' she whispered, 'I have no doubts about you. None at all.'

Greg took a deep breath. 'Good,' he murmured, 'So now maybe I can tell you some things I've had on my mind for a few days. Like——'

He broke off as Susan suddenly wriggled free of his arms and smoothed her shirt and muttered, 'Somebody's coming.'

He swung his head and saw two white-jacketed figures strolling towards them. It was David and Jimmy, and they had come quite close before Susan had spotted them behind Greg.

Under his breath, Greg muttered an oath, then took her arm and they strolled casually towards the two approaching men.

When they reached each other Jimmy said, 'Everyone seems to have the same idea—a pre-bedtime stroll around my ancestral home.'

Greg made some kind of reply and Susan smiled at Jimmy and David. Jimmy looked keenly at her and said, 'I'm glad to see you look better, Susan. You did look a little tired when you left the table.'

She nodded. 'Yes, I feel much better now. The walk seemed to clear my head.'

David looked at her briefly but said nothing as Jimmy went on, 'Somewhere tucked away in my private quarters I have a bottle of very excellent cognac. When my esteemed parents are away I occasionally have a snifter before retiring. I would be very honoured, Greg, if you would join David and me—and of course you too, Susan.'

Susan demurred, but Jimmy waved his hand imperiously. 'Come on, Susan. I thought I was being very non-chauvinist, inviting a lady into a male sanctum. I'm not excluding you because of your sex, so you should leap at the chance of relaxing with three males in a masculine atmosphere of brandy and cigars!'

His eyebrows lifted as he waited for her reply.

She sighed and forced a smile. It was difficult to refuse Jimmy after the lavish hospitality he regularly bestowed on the company's clients. She knew Jimmy refused to accept any payment for having the tourists stay at the palace, much as David had tried to put it on a commercial footing.

She said, 'I'd love to join you, Jimmy. I'm flattered to be asked to be one of the boys.'

He glanced over her curving figure and commented, 'I don't think you could ever pass as one of the boys, Susan.' Then he smiled and said, 'And you, Greg—I insist you join us. It's only ten o'clock and I never feel like bed until midnight.'

Greg nodded. 'It'll be a pleasure.'

They strolled back to the palace, and with Jimmy giving the lead, conversation flowed easily and the slight strain that had existed when they had first come upon each other quickly evaporated.

In his comfortable study in the family wing, Jimmy poured cognac for the two men and himself, after first pouring a glass of wine for Susan, who had never developed a taste for brandy. Then he passed cigars around and the three men lit up. Neither David nor Greg normally smoked, but on a special occasion like this they both accepted a cigar.

Jimmy sat alongside Susan on a big leather couch while David and Greg sat on either side in matching armchairs. At first, it was a slightly frustrating experience for Susan. She would much rather not have been interrupted when she had been in Greg's arms and he had been about to tell her about the things he had on his mind. But Jimmy was a skilled conversationalist and he loved having company, especially the company of well-travelled people from other countries.

He had placed the brandy bottle on a low table in front of them, apologising that he couldn't keep alcohol in decanters as he'd have liked to. 'My esteemed father would quickly spot a decanter. So I'm forced to hide my liquor at the back of cupboards and in other places, rather like Ray Milland in that old movie. *The Lost Weekend!*'

Jimmy was a movie buff, and loved old movies. There was a projection room at the palace where

sixteen-millimetre copies of old and new films were
regularly shown.

During the leisurely conversation, Susan glanced
covertly at Greg once or twice as, on Jimmy's
prompting, he talked about the political and econ-
omic situation in the United States. Greg returned
her glance, but with David watching closely, he
kept his face expressionless.

Once, when David was re-lighting his cigar, and
Jimmy was pouring himself another brandy, Greg
managed to meet her eyes, and he gave her a smile
of such intimate warmth that her heart turned over
and she had to breathe deeply to stop herself
trembling. His smile had said, 'The night's not over
yet. Soon we'll be alone together.'

It was almost midnight before they broke up.
Protocol decreed that the guests shouldn't express
any desire to leave the young heir's presence. They
had to wait for him, although Jimmy rarely stood
on protocol and had taken no offence when Susan
had left the banqueting table earlier in the evening.

But finally he suggested they all probably wanted
to retire. He said it rather wistfully, as if he would
have been happy to have stayed up drinking and
talking longer. But they all agreed it was time they
should leave, and after saying goodnight, Greg and
David escorted Susan to the old harem wing.

After mounting the wide staircase, they came
first to Greg's suite and David said, as they paused
outside, 'If it's not too late for you, Greg, there are
a couple of small points I'd like to discuss with
you. About your new tour plans.'

Greg hesitated and looked at Susan. He said,

'Well, I am just a little weary, David.'

'It won't take long,' David said with un-characteristic forcefulness. 'I'd like to ring K.K. early in the morning about the matter, but there's just two small points you could guide me on. Five minutes would be enough.'

Greg smothered a sigh then forced a smile. 'O.K., five minutes.' He opened the door and stood aside for David to go in.

Susan murmured, 'Well, I'll say goodnight.'

'Goodnight, Susan,' David called as he went past Greg into the suite.

Greg glanced quickly at David's back, then whispered to Susan, 'See you soon—I'll come to your room.'

She nodded and returned his smile, then walked to her room. As she went in she reflected that David had gone out of his way to prevent Greg and her from being alone. And when he did leave Greg and come to his own room he would be right next door. They would have to be very subdued with David so close.

Then she brightened. What did it matter? The main thing was that Greg loved her. She was sure of that, and she was certain he would tell her so—tonight.

Half an hour ticked past before she heard David enter his room. So much for his five minutes! she thought as she listened to him moving around next door.

Another half hour of keyed-up waiting passed before she heard the lightest of taps on her door. She tiptoed across and opened it quietly; Greg slipped inside and took her in his arms and kissed her.

'It's been agony,' he muttered, and one finger flew to her lips as she shushed him.

'David's next door,' she whispered, 'and the walls are very thin.'

He lowered his voice. 'I know he's next door. He told me so. That's why it's been agony, because I waited until he's asleep—I hope.'

With one arm around her, he glanced round the tiny room. 'This is like a nun's cell,' he murmured. 'And in my place there's a living room and a bedroom—with a big double bed.'

'We can't go to your room,' she whispered. 'The servants might see us.'

'They might have seen me,' he muttered. He rolled his eyes. 'This is ridiculous! I feel like I'm in a French farce.'

Susan stifled a giggle. 'I feel as if I'm back in boarding school!'

He raised an eyebrow. 'Oh? You mean you used to have guys in your room at school?'

She prodded him gently. 'No. But the bed here's just as narrow, although it's a little more comfortable.'

Greg glanced at her small bed, then at the single timber-framed easy chair. 'We've got no choice,' he murmured. 'We'll have to use your bed.'

'To sit on!' she whispered reprovingly.

She tiptoed over to the bed and sat down carefully. He followed and lowered himself beside her, but under his weight the bed creaked alarmingly.

'Shh!' she breathed as he took her in his arms.

The bed creaked again as they moved on it.

'Oh, to hell with this!' Greg whispered loudly. 'We're going to my room.' He got to his feet. 'Come on!'

Susan let him pull her to her feet and he led her by the hand to the door which he opened and then peered carefully along the corridor outside. 'The coast is clear,' he muttered. 'No servants around.'

She stifled a giggle. 'It *is* like a French farce!'

He put a finger to his lips as they crept into the corridor and Susan gently pulled her door closed behind her.

They reached his suite and slipped inside, and with a huge sigh of relief he closed the door behind them.

'Praise the lord!' he sighed. 'Now we can talk normally. But not too loud,' he added, glancing towards a door on the right. 'That's a communicating door. I think the number one wife's handmaiden used to sleep through there.'

'Who's in there now?' asked Susan, still keeping her voice low.

He shrugged. 'I don't know. The door's locked on the other side. I checked it.'

The living room was opulently furnished with heavy teak and mahogany furniture. But the two-seater settee he led her over to wasn't especially comfortable.

'I think the seats are stuffed with horsehair,' he said as he sat down and drew her down beside him. 'The harem wives sure led spartan lives. They were probably very happy to get invited into the Sultan's bed for the night. Not that there's anything wrong with my bed,' he added. 'Would you like to see it?' He nodded towards another door on the left.

'Not at the moment,' she murmured as she melted into his arms. 'It's so nice to be alone with you—at last.'

Greg bent his head and kissed her lingeringly. Then he took his lips away and said softly, 'This has been the darndest tour.'

She murmured, 'And this is its last night.'

'Yes,' he breathed. 'And I wouldn't have believed I could have had so much trouble, just to have you to myself for one night.'

She confessed, 'I'm glad I've never made assignations with other men when I've been touring. It would have been impossible.'

Greg smiled as he stroked her hair. 'It's not usually so difficult to have an—assignation, when you're travelling.'

Susan sat up. 'Oh? Then you do this kind of thing often?'

He grinned. 'Not often, although I'll confess I haven't lived a monastic life on my travels. But this is different.'

'Why?'

He smiled. 'Well, it's the first time I've ever had a girl in my room in a harem. In fact, it's the first time I've ever been in a harem.'

'But you like it, don't you?'

He grinned. 'I admit I do. But there's another reason why it's different——'

'Hmm?'

He nuzzled her cheek. 'Because I'm with you.' His lips covered hers and she melted back into his arms as he embraced her. 'You're very beautiful,' he whispered, 'and I want you very much.'

'Want me?'

'And need you. You've dominated my thoughts since that first moment when you slid out of the minibus in Singapore. You looked all hot and bothered—but very, very attractive.'

He kissed her again and she squirmed happily against his shoulder.

'You were very mean to me that first day,' she told him. 'You were a very bad tourist. I'd never have guessed you were thinking about me that way.'

'I was preoccupied,' he explained. 'And I wasn't enjoying Singapore, until you came along. It was too stuffy and British.'

'I'm British,' she reminded him, cocking her head. 'Do you think I'm stuffy?'

He shook his head. 'No, you're delightfully un-stuffy. And——' he kissed her—'you certainly don't have a stiff upper lip! Or a lower one either.'

He kissed her again and she relaxed against him as he stroked her cheek. His fingers traced the line of her neck, then went slowly down her shirt front and lightly teased the cleft of her bosom.

She clutched him to her as his hand slid inside her shirt and found her bra top. 'Hmm,' he murmured, 'you're wearing a bra tonight?'

'Hmm. Sometimes I do, sometimes I don't.'

Gently he undid the buttons of her shirt and as he kissed her his hand played with the fastening of her bra.

'Does this come off?' he queried softly.

'Sometimes. And quite easily if I breathe in.'

She took a deep breath and he unsnapped her bra, then gently eased her shirt from her shoulders and drew her bra away. He kissed her passionately, then his head sank on to her bosom and she clutched him tightly. Ecstasy overwhelmed her as his lips caressed her breasts while his warm hands stroked her back, tracing the line of her spine to its base.

He raised his head and she pulled his face up close to hers, then kissed him lingeringly.

Greg murmured, 'And I thought all English girls were cold!'

'I thought I was too,' she whispered, 'until I met you.'

Greg smiled. 'My darling. You're the most——' He stopped as he saw her eyes widen as she stared over his shoulder. There was the sound of a door opening and he swung his head round as the communicating door was flung back and Tanya stood there in a short apricot nightgown.

He sprang up, and Susan's face flamed as she feverishly covered her naked bosom. She stared at Tanya as Greg got to his feet, his brow black.

Tanya put one hand to her mouth and expressed astonished embarrassment. 'Oh!' she cried. 'I'm so sorry, Greg! I didn't realise you had—company.'

Susan struggled to her feet, her face scarlet with mortification.

Greg snapped, 'I didn't know Tanya was next door!'

'Liar!' Susan cried. 'I bet you asked for this cosy little arrangement!' She pulled on her shirt and clutching her bra she made towards the door.

'Susan!' he growled. 'Wait——'

She wrenched the door open, then turned, eyes blazing, face flaming, and cried, 'You really *do* like being in a harem, don't you! Well, I'm not going to join in your little orgy! I think you're—you're—Oh, you're an *animal*!'

He stared at her icily as she flounced out of the room. As she went, she heard Tanya say, 'I'm so sorry, Greg. I really didn't——'

Susan slammed the door behind her with a bang that echoed along the silent corridor. But she was past caring if anyone came out and saw her.

CHAPTER ELEVEN

NEXT morning, Susan found she couldn't get out of attending the village wedding. A major reason was that the bridegroom was a relative of Munir's, and he would have been disappointed, even insulted, if she hadn't come. A second reason was that she was needed to translate the ceremony, which was in Malay, for the benefit of her passengers.

It was the final day of the tour and all the passengers were in high spirits. Their stopover at the palace, and Jimmy's unflagging hospitality, had made a wonderful climax to the tour. Susan told them they would find the village wedding, and the feast that would follow, every bit as interesting. She explained that traditional weddings were often staged for tourists, but this was a real wedding they would take part in. They would also find quite a contrast between the simple village life and life at the Palace, although the village hospitality would be just as genuine and the welcome as sincere as Jimmy had given them.

Munir drove the coach to the kampong, which was only a short distance from the Palace. David followed in the Mercedes with Tanya and Greg. Jimmy, as the Sultan's son, was an important guest at the wedding and he was driven to the kampong by a liveried chauffeur. He rode in an early-model

Rolls-Royce, which was immaculately maintained. He wore traditional dress of white trousers and a richly-brocaded coat with a tasselled tarboosh on his head.

For the sake of her passengers, Susan made a determined effort to overcome her own misery. She had been able to avoid seeing Greg at breakfast by having some pineapple and papaya from the basket in her room. That, with the early morning tea which the servants brought to every guestroom, was enough for her, because she didn't feel like eating.

She saw David briefly while she was assembling the passengers to board the coach. He was in high spirits, for during his discussions with Greg the previous night they had worked out preliminary details of a contract between Trans Asia Tours and Tiger Tours. David had talked to K.K. on the phone early in the morning, and K.K. was as pleased as David that there would now be no need to bring any outside investor into the company.

David looked at her closely. 'You don't seem terribly happy. It's a wonderful break for us. The company—me—and you.'

Susan forced a smile. 'I—I'm just a little tired. I'm beginning to think I may have had enough of tour conducting. Three years of constant travelling becomes wearing.'

He nodded. 'For tour escorting, three years is a long time. But——' he brightened—'this could be a good time to start thinking of changing your lifestyle.' He squeezed her hand. 'As I said last night—marrying me, for example.'

She turned her head slightly to avoid his eyes. Then she saw Greg and Tanya walking down the wide stairway from the palace. David swivelled his head and saw them and waved.

He said quickly, 'But we'll talk about us later—tonight in Penang, when the tour is over.'

Susan nodded, and he released her hand and strode over to join Greg and Tanya.

In the coach on the way to the kampong Susan gave the passengers some facts about Malay traditions, and this helped keep her mind off last night with Greg until they reached the village.

As the passengers disembarked, the Malay headman came forward to welcome them.

'Selamat datang!' he said, bowing to Susan, and she bowed and returned the Malay greeting.

Politely she exchanged news with him and they told each other what had happened since she had last been at the village with a tour three weeks ago.

The headman and Munir were both involved with preparations for the wedding, so Susan took her charges on a tour of the village. Mainly, the villagers existed in the traditional way, living in thatched-roofed huts on stilts, built over the edge of a large pond. They fished in the well-stocked pond and its stream, grew some crops and kept a few domestic animals. They wove their own simple clothes and were self-sufficient in most things.

After the tour, Susan shepherded her passengers to the village centre where the wedding was about to get under way. A raised dais had been built and decorated with poles holding arches of colourful flowers and orchids. The villagers assembled in a big horseshoe-shaped circle around a long table which faced the dais.

The table was for guests from outside the village, mainly Susan's group. Jimmy sat in the middle of the table and he sat Greg on his right and David on his left. The tourists sat behind the table on either side of Jimmy. Tanya knelt on a cushion on the ground about half way along on Jimmy's left while Susan knelt similarly on a cushion half way along on his right.

Both girls faced the guests and from their positions they could turn their heads and watch the ceremony, then turn back and translate and comment on what took place. They spoke quietly so as not to disturb the ceremony.

The groom was a slim, brown-faced boy who looked about fourteen and the bride was a willowy, almond-eyed girl who looked even younger.

They were dressed in traditional wedding robes, heavy with brocade and gold and silver thread. The boy looked stiff and uncomfortable, but the girl was shyly radiant.

The ceremony was a lengthy one, and as she knelt on her cushion, Susan was conscious of Greg's gaze on her, but she resolutely avoided looking at him, confining the arc of her eyes to Maimie Eikhorn, who was sitting beside Greg.

As the bride and groom were finally joined in matrimony, Susan felt her eyes become misty and her commentary tailed off. She cast one covert glance at Greg from under moist lashes and his eyes met hers, boring into her. She felt her heart turn over and got quickly to her feet as young vil-

lage girls came round the table distributing to each
guest a decorated, gilt-encrusted egg on a stick. The
eggs, which were traditional at the ceremony, were
beautifully done, encrusted with tiny beads over
colourful, painted designs, and much larger than
chicken eggs.

At the edge of the village, under big shady
banyan trees, tables laden with food had been set
out and the bride and groom were escorted to the
place of honour and the wedding feast commenced.
The tour group were given places among the villagers and it was a very happy, festive occasion.

Susan was kept busy moving around translating
for the passengers as they tried to converse with
the villagers, many of whom spoke little English.

During the feast, everyone began dancing, and
the villagers tried to teach the visitors some of the
traditional steps. There was a great deal of hilarity
and everyone was thoroughly enjoying themselves.

Susan thought she must be the only unhappy
person at the wedding, but she tried hard not to
show it. She went out of her way to avoid getting
too close to Greg, especially as Tanya stayed near
his side most of the time. Tanya held his arm and
laughed and chatted gaily. He didn't seem to mind
her display of affection, Susan thought bitterly as
she turned her head away and painfully recalled
last night in Greg's room.

He was really insatiable, she thought anguishedly. Obviously he had known Tanya was in
the adjoining room. He would have got Jimmy to
arrange that. No doubt she had already visited him
in his room during the afternoon when Susan had

been helping Jimmy show the tourists round the palace. And then he'd decided it was Susan's turn. Unless—her face flamed—unless he had arranged for Tanya to break in on them with the idea of taking them both into his bedroom so he could loll back like a Sultan with two women in his bed! She wouldn't put it past him. For he hadn't once said he felt any emotion for her stronger than mere desire.

She shrugged morosely. Obviously he didn't love her. Obviously he didn't really care about her. He'd merely planned to use her for an amusing interlude on a tour that probably bored him. She sniffed and turned her head, to meet Jimmy's enquiring gaze. He nodded to the headman he had been conversing with, and the headman salaamed as Jimmy left him and strolled over to Susan.

She forced a smile and said brightly, 'I think this might be a good time to say goodbye, Jimmy. And thank you once again for your wonderful hospitality.'

He drew her aside under a banyan tree and said softly, 'I was watching you for a while, and you look very sad. Have you had a quarrel with David?'

She shook her head vigorously. 'Oh, no! David's very happy.'

'Yes. Forgive a personal question—but will we be seeing another wedding soon?'

She shook her head, confused. 'I—I don't know. I mean, I'm not sure. I——'

Over his shoulder she saw Greg and Tanya dancing a formal Malay dance, and Greg's eyes caught Susan's as she stared at him. Jimmy glanced round and intercepted their exchange.

He looked back at Susan. 'Hmm,' he murmured, 'I get the picture.' Then he struck his forehead with one hand. 'Lord, did I get things all wrong! I carefully put David in the room next to you, then I later placed Tanya next to Greg, thinking that would be the arrangement that would please everyone.' He smiled wryly. 'I made quite a boo-boo, didn't I?'

'Oh!' she said helplessly.

Jimmy nodded. 'Well, I've done my duty and had a formal dance with the bride. So now I must go and dance with some of the guests.' He smiled and squeezed her hand. 'I'll say goodbye before you leave.'

Susan stared at him as he walked over to the dancers and very smoothly took Tanya by the hand, after bowing to Greg, who relinquished Tanya and grinned at Jimmy as he led her into the circle of dancers.

Then Greg glanced up and caught Susan's eyes as she stared at him. She gulped and ran forward. She stopped a pace away from him and said in a rush, 'I'm sorry, I—I thought you'd arranged to have Tanya next to you last night. I—I didn't——'

He looked at her flushed face, his brow dark, then he said bitingly, 'I really have no interest in what you think, Miss York. Or in any of your misconceptions. You bore me. So goodbye—and excuse me.'

He turned and strode away towards where David was standing and began to speak to him.

Susan bit her lip and turned her head away, to meet Munir's eyes. He looked at her sympathetically.

He came over and said, 'I think it's time to get everyone on board the coach if we want to reach Penang before dark.' He cocked his head and glanced up at the sky. 'Also we're going to get a heavy downpour soon.'

She nodded and said she would start calling everyone on board as soon as the dance stopped.

Munir glanced over at Greg, deep in conversation with David. He said, 'It has not been a very happy tour for you, Susan, has it?'

She squared her shoulders. 'That's the second time I've been told that today. Do I look so miserable?'

Munir smiled. 'Well, you don't look your usual happy self.'

David left Greg and strode up and joined Susan and Munir. He said, 'As this is the final leg, Greg wants to ride in the coach so he can talk to the passengers and get their comments on the tour. It'll be useful when he's putting his own tours together. I'd like to be with him when he talks with them, so Tanya can follow us in the car.'

Susan said quickly, 'I'd rather drive the car. Tanya can take my place in the coach.'

He raised one eyebrow.

She hurried on, 'I—I'm really tired. I'd be glad to be on my own for a couple of hours. I'll go ahead of the coach and be waiting when you all arrive. Then I can say my goodbyes.'

He nodded. 'O.K., if that's how you'd like it. I'll

tell Tanya to take over and get everyone aboard.'

'I'll help round them up,' she said, 'then I'll take the car.' She glanced up at the sky which had darkened in the last few minutes. 'It's going to pour soon.'

Under the lowering sky, the villagers quickly began carrying left-over food into the huts while Susan hurried round telling her charges to board the coach.

They were all on board as the first heavy drops of rain began to fall. Tanya got in and took Susan's jump seat facing the passengers. David and Greg were the last to get on board, and Greg looked at Susan and said, 'So you're not coming with us?' His expression was cool and distant.

'No,' she said, avoiding his eyes, 'I have to drive the car.

He shrugged, then swung himself into the coach, David following. The door closed behind them with a hiss.

Susan dashed across the clearing from where the coach was standing towards the Mercedes as rain suddenly started to pour down in sheets. She wrenched the car door open and dived in, her uniform skirt and blouse soaked after only a few seconds in the torrent.

She wound the window up and sat, shaking rain off herself. The downpour was so heavy she couldn't see more than three feet out of the windows which quickly misted up in the tropical heat. She made to start the motor to use the demister when she realised she didn't have the keys. David had forgotten to give them to her.

'Oh, blast!' she muttered.

With the noise of the rain lashing on the car roof, she couldn't hear if the coach had taken off, nor could she see if it had gone. The only way to get the keys was to go back out into the teeming rain and try to attract Munir's attention if he hadn't already moved off. Which meant she'd end by being completely soaked—with a two-hour drive ahead of her. A sure way to catch a chill— and maybe pneumonia! A fitting end to a miserable tour, she thought bitterly.

She was about to open the door when the handle was suddenly wrenched from her hand and the door flew open, then a very drenched Greg dived in on top of her, crying out, 'Move over before I drown!'

He sprawled on top of her as she tried to disentangle herself from him. Finally she struggled across to the passenger side as he slid behind the wheel and pulled the door shut.

He shook himself like a dog, water spraying from his dripping hair all over her.

'Hey!' Susan protested. 'You're soaking me!'

'That makes two of us,' he muttered as he undid his saturated shirt and peeled it off. He turned and spread it over the back of the seat. Then he fished in his pants pocket and brought out the key which he inserted in the ignition. He started the motor then turned on the heater-demister.

'Thank you,' Susan said shortly. 'I'm sorry to delay you. I expect you'll have to wait until the rain eases before you can get back on the coach.'

He shook his head as he started the windshield

wipers. 'The coach has gone. I'll drive us to Penang.'

She stared at him. 'I thought you wanted to go with the coach? To talk to the passengers?'

He said gravely, 'I wanted to ride on the coach to talk with you. I thought Tanya and David might have taken the car, but it didn't work out that way.'

She turned her head away. 'I don't know what you would want to talk to me about. I don't think we have anything to say to each other.'

Greg nodded. 'I agree. There are more important things than talking.' He slid over close to her and she backed away against her door, but he pinned her in his arms, pulling her tight against his bare chest.

She struggled in his grip, but she could have saved herself the effort as he forced her head back and kissed her soundly on the lips.

She kicked and struggled, but he held her tightly. Finally he took his lips from hers and smiled down at her.

'For once,' he said, 'we won't be interrupted. Only a nut would be outside in this rain.'

He glanced through the windshield, where it was impossible to see the nose of the car through the lashing torrent. He released her, then moved away slightly and undid his belt, opened his sodden trousers and raised himself on the seat as he began to slip out of them.

'What are you doing?' she cried, her breasts heaving.

'Taking off my pants,' he said calmly. 'They're

soaked, and I'm not going to sit around and get a chill.'

He slid his trousers down over his legs, then pulled them off, tugging his shoes off as he did so.

Susan stared at him, naked except for his pants, and gulped. 'You can't do that!' she protested. 'What will it look like when the rain stops?'

He shrugged. 'Nobody's going to see. I'll start driving when the rain stops. Then, when my clothes are dried out, I'll stop and put them on again.'

'*I'm* going to drive!' she snapped, still panting from his embrace and kiss. 'This is a company car—and only company personnel can drive company vehicles.'

Greg smiled as he ran his hand through his wet hair. 'I think this is where I came in,' he drawled. 'We had this argument before, remember?'

She swung her head away sharply. His near-nakedness in the steamed-up, intimate atmosphere of the closed car was very disturbing.

He said conversationally, 'I think it's time we put our cards on the table and you admitted that you love me.'

She jerked her head to face him and gaped. 'Oh——' she began, but he leaned towards her and she began to struggle as he took her in his arms again.

'I love you,' he murmured. 'Very much. I thought I did, almost from the first time we met. But watching that beautiful wedding today clinched it. I'd like us to have a wedding like that.'

'Oh!' She stared into his eyes as he drew her gently to him and kissed her very tenderly.

He kissed her for a long time, then suddenly she was kissing him back and clinging to him and telling him she loved him. All her pent-up love and desire flooded from her, and suddenly the car seemed to be filled with brilliant sunshine.

Finally she opened her eyes and found that the sun *was* shining. The brief tropical downpour had ceased as suddenly as it had begun.

She said shakily, 'Oh, my darling!'

Greg grinned as he embraced her. 'Now,' he said, 'for the first and last time in our lives together, I'm going to let you have the last word.' He paused and looked into her eyes. 'But it's a very significant word.' He stroked her cheek, then asked, 'Will you marry me?'

Susan looked deep into his warm eyes and sighed.

'Oh, yes,' she murmured. 'Yes!'

Harlequin® Plus

THE LUXURY OF SILK

The soft touch of silk next to the skin is one luxury that many Harlequin heroines—in fact, most women—find irresistible. And fabrics woven from silk have been around for centuries, with some of history's most magnificent costumes fashioned from it—first in the orient and later in Europe. The ancients are said to have prized it highly, often exchanging silk, weight for weight, for pure gold.

The silk industry reached Europe in the twelfth century, first in Sicily and later in Italy, France and Spain. Silk was not manufactured in England, however, until 1605, when some skilled French refugees established themselves there.

Silk owes its beginning to the lowly silkworm, of course, a creature indigenous to China. The silkworm is, in fact, a small caterpillar that hatches from the egg of a species of moth. Like any other caterpillar, it is virtually an eating machine, growing rapidly in size as it munches its way through leaf after leaf. When fat and fully grown, the silkworm secretes liquid silk, which solidifies around the worm to form a cocoon.

Man learned long ago to separate the soft silk from the silkworm—by immersing the cocoon in hot water—then to spin it into thread and weave the thread into fabric. Now a highly sophisticated industry with millions of commercial silkworms feasting on mounds of mulberry leaves, the process of silk-making is fascinating—and extremely profitable. Today, the world's chief silk-manufacturing nations are China, Japan, Korea, Italy and the Soviet Union, but fortunate wearers are women the world over.